GRANNY UNDERCOVER

A SECRET AGENT GRANNY MYSTERY BOOK 2

HARPER LIN

M
LIN   '17

AUG

This is a work of fiction. Names, characters, organizations, places, events, and incidents are either products of the author's imagination or are used fictitiously.

GRANNY UNDERCOVER

ISBN-13: 978-1987859478

ISBN-10: 1987859472

www.harperlin.com

CONTENTS

ONE

I never thought I'd discover a murder while inspecting peat moss.

It's not that I'm unused to violent death. After all, I've caused enough of it in my day. It's just that peat moss and near decapitation have never been associated in my mind. Rather, I think of suburban gardens. As for decapitation, I associate it with less pleasant parts of the globe. I guess I just need to have a more open attitude about the world.

I'm Barbara Gold. Age: seventy. Height: five-five. Eyes: blue. Hair: gray. Weight: none of your business. Specialties: undercover surveillance, small arms, chemical weapons, Middle Eastern and Latin American politics. Current status: retired widow and grandmother.

Addendum to current status: realizing that retirement can be a lot less boring than I feared it would be.

So I was standing in the Cheerville Gardening Centre, trying to figure out what variety of peat moss I needed for the flower bed I was planning, or even if I needed peat moss at all, when I happened to overhear an interesting conversation.

"Happened to overhear" may be a bit misleading. I heard two women whispering in the next aisle, and I immediately tuned in. Whispered conversations were always the most interesting conversations, even if they happened in a place as banal as the Cheerville Gardening Centre.

"Centre," not "Center." The place had an English theme, complete with a fake Big Ben sticking out of the roof and portraits of fox hunts on the walls. I suspected no self-respecting English-person would be caught dead going into a place with such décor.

Anyway, back to the whispered conversation coming from a pair of gray-haired ladies, one in her late sixties and the other well into her eighties.

"After what happened to poor Archibald, I can't bear to use hedge clippers anymore," said the younger one. The fact that she said this in a fearful whisper is what caught my attention.

The older woman's voice also dropped to a whisper. "What happened, exactly? All I heard was that he cut himself."

"Oh, if it were only that," the younger woman said in an eager sotto voce. "He was pruning his hedges, getting ready for the lawn show, when he hit some sort of knot in the wood or something. The hedge clippers sprang back on him, cut his forehead, and then dug into his neck. He was nearly decapitated."

"You don't say?" the older woman replied. She sounded thrilled. Not thrilled that Archibald, whoever he was, was dead, but thrilled she was getting a juicy bit of gossip.

The younger woman continued in a whisper. Despite their advanced age, neither of them seemed to have any problems with their hearing. Their ears had probably been sharpened by a lifetime of whispering juicy tidbits about their neighbors.

"Yes, nearly cut off. They found him on his lawn, simply covered in blood."

"Oh dear. I suppose someone else will win in the topiary category this year," the older one said.

I immediately knew dear old Archibald's death hadn't been an accident, but murder. Hedge clippers had a safety switch. If you didn't keep a button on the handle pressed down, the clippers turned off.

Lawn mowers had the same thing. This was to prevent accidents from getting any worse. Thus, if the dead topiary champion had really slipped and cut his forehead with the hedge clippers—an unlikely event in the first place—he would have let go of the switch and wouldn't have been able to nearly decapitate himself. Hedge clippers were specifically designed so accidents like that could not happen.

Of course, there was always the possibility of suicide, but I found that doubtful. There were easier ways to kill yourself than decapitation, and I'm not sure even the most determined man bent on annihilation could keep the safety switch pressed as hedge clippers sawed through his neck.

So the far more likely explanation for the world being short one gardener was that he was murdered.

The two ladies were moving away, pushing a shopping cart filled with seed packets and a pair of metal watering cans with scenes of English country cottages painted on the sides.

After abandoning my shopping for the moment, I tailed them to the checkout, but their conversation had turned to other things. Once they had made their purchases, I followed them out of the

Cheerville Gardening Centre and noted the license plate of their car. I probably wouldn't need it, but any intel could be useful intel. Then I strolled back into the building to finish making my purchases. After I had done that, I would pay a visit to the police chief. I found myself whistling a happy tune. There was something satisfying about getting involved in a murder case. It made me feel young.

But the murder would have to wait an hour or so because I was on a mission. I'd had a lot of tough missions in my life—Kandahar, Medellín, Mogadishu—but this was one of the toughest. It was beyond my training, beyond even my secondary skill set. I was entering a dangerous, unknown territory fraught with peril.

I was taking up gardening.

Heading back to my shopping cart, or "shopping trolley" as it was labeled—apparently, that was what they were called in England—I examined the contents. Trays of various types of flowers ready for transplanting into my garden? Check. Plain watering can with no embarrassing image on the side? Check. Trowel? Check. Pruning shears? Check. Gloves adorned with a blindingly-cheerful floral print? Check. One copy of *Gardening for Numbskulls*? Check. Was the copy of *Gardening for Numb-*

skulls buried under all that other stuff so no one saw it and laughed at me? Check.

I thought I had everything, but did I need peat moss? I had heard somewhere that you needed peat moss for a garden, although to be perfectly honest, I wasn't even sure what peat moss was made of. I could recite the chemical makeup of plastic explosive at the drop of a hat, but peat moss? No idea.

Gardening was something I'd never had time for, or even an interest in, during my career. James and I were always being called away on missions. We never knew when we'd have to leave or how long we'd be gone. It would have been impossible to maintain a garden. How we ever raised our son, Frederick, without him turning into some basketcase alcoholic is beyond me. My parents did much of his parenting for us, something I'd always felt guilty about, although Frederick had never held it against us, bless his heart.

But now, my life was radically different. No more infiltrating enemy bases. No more hunting down narcotraffickers. No more blowing up illegal weapons factories. These days, I was living a quiet, peaceful life in a quiet, peaceful neighborhood in a quiet, peaceful town. I wouldn't have been caught dead in a place like Cheerville if my son and his family didn't live here. Once I retired and James passed, I realized I wanted to be near them. The town was still frightfully dull, however.

"Thank God for murder," I muttered.

"May I help you, madam?" someone asked from behind me.

I nearly jumped out of my skin. Whirling around, I saw a young man of about college age dressed like an English butler, complete with bowler hat.

"Is there something you require?" he asked in an English accent.

Cheerville Gardening Centre took its English theme way too far. All the employees were dressed like the servants in *Upstairs, Downstairs*—or *Downton Abbey* for you youngsters—and they were all actually English. Most were young, and I think the management must have hired every single English student from the local university to work there.

Getting over my surprise and irritation at having been sneaked up on—and hoping he hadn't heard that bit about murder—I asked, "I was wondering if I need peat moss. I'm planning a flower garden, you see, as well as sprucing up a few bushes in my front lawn, but I've never done this sort of thing before. Do I need some peat moss?"

"Ah, yes, madam," he said with the kind of courtesy no one under thirty ever uses unless they're paid to. "Peat moss is most efficacious in adding nutrients to the soil and helping it to retain water. I suppose your garden has not been tended for some time?"

"Not since I've owned it."

"I see. Then it would be best to enrich the soil as much as possible. Might I suggest some growth pellets as well?"

"Growth pellets?"

"Concentrated pellets you put under the plant. They're made of condensed nutrients that will help your plants grow. If you're starting a flower garden this late in the season, it might be a good idea to use them if you wish to have a proper display by summer. They also help the flowers survive being transplanted, which is a shock for any plant."

"Oh, I see. How do I get them under the plants?"

The kid's serene expression faltered, and a smile tugged at the sides of his mouth. It took him a moment to recover. He'd never make it as a butler at a fine country estate.

"You need to dig a hole for each plant in your bed. Your flower bed, that is." I thought this clarification rather insulting and was tempted to give him a karate chop that would snap his clavicle. "Make it slightly larger than you need. Put the growth pellet at the bottom, then some peat moss, then the flower with most of the soil from the pot. Then add a bit of peat moss around the sides to fill it in. Would you like me to pick out a basic gardening manual? There's one called *Gardening for N*—"

"That's quite all right, thank you," I said, grabbing a bag of peat moss and adding it to my cart. It weighed twenty pounds, and my back twinged as I put it in, but I wasn't about to allow this rude little boy a chance to help me again.

I hate not being in the know. In my line of work, not knowing something could get you killed. It certainly got a lot of my coworkers killed. I'd have to spend some time with the book and plant the flowers tomorrow once I knew what I was doing. Hopefully, they'd last that long. I wasn't sure they would, but I'd have to risk it.

I got out of the Cheerville Gardening Centre with no further humiliation and left Big Ben in the dust. As I drove back home through Cheerville's leafy, orderly streets, I started thinking about Archibald's grisly encounter with the hedge clippers. Why would someone choose such a nasty murder weapon? Was it because Archibald was a gardener, and the murderer wanted to make a point? Or perhaps it was a spur-of-the-moment killing, and the hedge clippers were the nearest thing to hand. Also, why were those two acquaintances of his assuming he had died by accident? Wouldn't the police have launched a murder investigation for such an obvious case?

My pulse was pounding. This was far more interesting than transplanting petunias or daffodils or whatever I had just bought. I didn't even know the names for most flowers. I simply picked out what I thought looked nice.

"Thank God for murder," I repeated out loud.

And cats.

I had never pictured myself growing old in a snoozy suburb, caring for a cat and pottering around a garden, but life had thrown me too many curveballs for me to be incapable of rolling with the punches. Even mixed metaphors didn't bother me anymore.

Dandelion was there to greet me, as she always was. She's a lovely little tortoiseshell kitten I had picked up a few weeks earlier while casing a pet shop. The young man who ran the shop was a local drug dealer who I suspected had been involved in a murder, and I had gone to the shop pretending to be interested in buying a kitten. I ended up leaving with Dandelion and several clues that helped me crack the case.

As soon as I opened the front door, Dandelion scooted out from under the sofa and shot straight for the door, hoping to get outside. My reaction time was still good enough to get the door closed behind me, but I worried one day she'd be too fast for me, or I'd squash her in the door. My grandson, Martin, would never forgive me. I would never forgive me. More to the point, Dandelion would never forgive me.

That cat yearned to go outside, which was why I had decided to start a garden—so that Dandelion would have a jungle where she could pretend to be a tiger. I'd already bought some netting to put around the fence so she couldn't slip out, but without a garden inside, it would look like Stalag 17. Dandelion would just have to wait until the garden was ready before I could let her safely play Queen of the Jungle.

"Good afternoon," I said as she crawled up my pant leg. This was another of her habits. I'd lost enough pairs of panty hose to her little claws that I'd learned to wear pants most of the time.

Taking advantage of her nearness as she hung on my leg, I scooped her up, endured several scratches from her tiny claws, and locked her in the kitchen. There was no way I could move all my gardening purchases out of the car without her shooting out the front door like a furry little meteor.

I brought in the *Gardening for Numbskulls* book and the tools then set the flowers on the front porch and watered them. Water leaked out the holes in the bottom of their little plastic boxes, making an unattractive puddle on my porch. By this time, Dandelion was mewling piteously and scratching at the kitchen door.

"Coming! Once I'm done, I'll feed you, and we can settle in for a cup of tea, all right?" I called. More quietly, I added, "Oh dear, I've reached the 'old lady who has conversations with her cat' phase. And now I'm talking to myself! I'll be pushing a shopping trolley down Main Street and muttering to myself before long."

Clamping my mouth shut, I opened the kitchen door and watched a tortoiseshell blur fly for the front door, veer off at the last moment when it became obvious the door was closed, and disappear under the sofa.

I opened a tin of cat food and made myself a cup of tea, already thinking about the murder I'd heard about. The thought got me so excited I almost didn't notice Dandelion munching contentedly from her bowl.

Within a few minutes, I'd settled down with a cup of tea in front of my computer and was scanning through the recent death notices in the *Cheerville Gazette*. There being so many retirees in Cheerville, it took some time to get through, but eventually, I found what I was looking for.

Beloved father and noted gardener Archibald Heaney of 67 Terrace Lane, Cheerville, died by accident at his home on the afternoon of Wednesday, April 12, in his garden in Cheerville. He was 84. A leading topiary expert, past president of the American Topiary Society, and contributor to its magazine Green Art, *Mr. Heaney was well known throughout the Cheerville community for his work promoting gardening and for his prize-winning displays at his home. He was also past president of the Cheerville Gardening Society and an active practitioner of yoga at the Cheerville Senior Center.*

Born August 13, 1932, he was a veteran of the Korean War, where he was decorated with the Bronze Star for valor, and worked as a mechanical engineer at Boeing for 35 years before retiring. His wife, Dorothy, preceded him in death in 2007. He is survived by their daughter, Ellen, and sons, Andrew and Chris. Memorial services will be held at Cheerville Methodist Church this Friday at 11 a.m. In lieu of flowers, the family requests that contributions be made to the Fresh Air Fund.

I bit my lip. The obituary told me very little. It

didn't even tell me what "topiary" was. A quick internet search informed me it was the art of cutting bushes into various decorative shapes.

That switched on a lightbulb in my head. I'd seen Archibald's home. Once, when out shopping in my first month in Cheerville with my daughter-in-law, Alicia, we'd passed a large home with a spacious front lawn. At least a dozen bushes had been cut into the likenesses of animals or strange geometric shapes. Alicia had pointed it out to me and said it was a local landmark. We'd passed it again later that year to see the Christmas lights. Good old Archibald had put on quite a show.

I scanned through the police pages and didn't see any mention of a murder investigation, although that didn't mean there wasn't one. It was strange, though, that there hadn't been any rumors of one. My reading group was full of gossips, and there hadn't been a peep about someone getting sliced open with hedge clippers. You'd think that sort of thing would make the rounds.

Dandelion leapt onto the keyboard, walked in a tight circle, and lay down, turning into a fuzzy, comatose blob. The screen displayed several pages of the *Cheerville Gazette* before freezing on one. In the box at the top of the screen where you type the URL address, the letter M repeated over and over.

Dandelion had stepped on the Caps Lock, and her chin was resting on the "m" key.

"Never mind, Dandelion. I'm done with the computer. It's time to pay a visit to my friend at the police station."

TWO

Television and movies only showed you three types of cops—the streetwise tough guy who broke all the rules, the wide-eyed rookie with a heart of gold who usually got killed, and the grizzled old chief who did things by the book.

Arnold Grimal, police chief of the City of Cheerville, didn't fit any of these stereotypes.

Arnold Grimal had had it easy. He'd always been a policeman in quiet suburban towns. I'd checked his background and discovered the only time he'd fired his gun on a call was to take down a rabid raccoon. To his credit, he did take it out in one shot. He'd been on the force for thirty years, and while he'd seen his share of robberies, drug addicts, and domestic violence, the vast majority of his career had been spent handing out parking tickets or directing traffic at the Fourth of July parade. I think I seriously upset his laid-back lifestyle when I discovered a murderer in my reading group. I know for a fact he nearly had a heart attack when the director of the Central Intelligence Agency called and told him to take me seriously.

And now I had to ruin his day yet again.

Police Chief Grimal was in his middle fifties, with a serious paunch that draped over his waistline so much I couldn't see his belt. His hair was going thin on top, and he compensated by having one of those thick moustaches that went out of style in the seventies for everyone but policemen. His nose and cheeks showed faint red splotches that hinted at an overindulgence in the one intoxicating drug that was legal in the United States.

Okay, I wasn't being very kind. When he invited me into his office, his handshake was firm, and his breath smelled of Chinese takeout, not booze. Under his direction, the Cheerville Police Department ran efficiently, and there had been few inroads of crime like so many suburban areas had suffered in recent years. Grimal wasn't a bad cop; he was simply a colorless man in a colorless job.

Grimal closed the door behind him so we could speak privately.

He sat down behind his desk, which was strewn with paperwork. One of those plastic nameplates set in a little brass holder uselessly informed guests who they were speaking to. The nameplate was one of those ugly brown ones that looked like it had been made in the eighties and had been sitting there ever since.

"So how can I help the CIA this afternoon?" he asked.

"Well, it's not really a CIA matter, but I was curious about the death of Archibald Heaney."

"Oh. I'm sorry, did you know him?"

"Um, no, but some acquaintances of mine did."

"It's a shame. He was an upstanding member of the community. Pity he didn't reach out for help."

"Help?"

"He committed suicide."

"Did he?" I replied, making a good impression of being surprised. "I thought he had an accident."

Grimal shook his head. "I'm afraid not. That would have been impossible with hedge clippers, anyway. There's a safety switch that prevents that from happening. The only way he could have died was by deliberately holding down the switch."

"I see. So he held the switch as the hedge clippers cut into him?"

Grimal inclined his head as if to acknowledge this was indeed unusual.

"I've seen stranger things. The man had determination. He was a decorated war veteran, after all. The guy might have been quiet and unassuming in his old age, but that didn't mean he still didn't have grit when it counted."

"Does the county coroner agree with this assessment?"

Grimal nodded and gestured toward his computer screen. "I got the report right here."

The way he said it didn't make it sound as if I was invited to take a look myself. I decided on a different tactic.

"So do you have any idea why he killed himself?"

Grimal shrugged. "His health was in decline—arthritis and a heart condition, according to his doctor. Several of his gardening friends said he was worried he wouldn't be able to keep up with his hobby because the arthritis was getting worse. Plus, he lost his wife a while back. The press is always focusing on teen suicide, and while that's a major problem, it's senior citizens who are actually more likely to kill themselves. They lose a spouse, their health starts to decline, and they can't participate in the hobbies that keep them going. They lose hope."

This was followed by a short silence. I supposed it was my turn to say something, but I couldn't think of anything. I had lost the dearest man in the world a few years ago and had felt adrift ever since. Moving to Cheerville had helped a bit, especially being close to my son, daughter-in-law, and lovely grandson, but I'd felt a bit useless. It was hard to switch from international operative to granny at the drop of a hat. That last murder investigation had really saved me from a growing sense of despair.

And now, I was looking for another one.

I didn't need Grimal to explain to me the loneliness and black pit of depression that can come with old age. I'd been fighting it ever since James passed. But even in my darkest moments, I had never considered the possibility of ending it all. That was quitting, and while I understood the temptation, I simply wasn't the kind of person who quit.

Something told me Archibald Heaney wasn't, either. He'd survived war, had a long career in a demanding field, and led an active retirement right up to the day of his death.

I thought about that for a moment. Grimal may have been a sheltered small-town cop, but he was no fool. He didn't buy the suicide story any more than I did, so why was he trying to convince me? And why cover up a murder? I couldn't think of any reason why the police chief would want the local topiary expert dead, although I had to admit I didn't know enough about either man to form any conclusions.

What I did know was that I wouldn't get any more satisfaction here. Grimal had clammed up. Archibald's death had been a suicide, and that was the end of it as far as he was concerned.

But it wasn't the end of it for me.

I thanked Grimal and made some sympathetic remarks about the poor old man I pretended to believe had killed himself, and then I said my good-byes and left. I had some investigating to do.

The first stop was the scene of the crime.

Terrace Lane, as its name suggested, was a flat strip of land along the side of a long, low ridge overlooking Cheerville. It was prime real estate thanks to its lovely view over the treetops and historic town center. In the autumn, everyone came up here to see the colors. Around Christmastime, the elaborate light displays the residents of Terrace Lane put up were visible from many parts of town.

I drove slowly, looking at the numbers on the mailboxes of the large Colonial-style houses. I needn't have bothered. It was obvious which house was Archibald Heaney's. As I passed a series of identical front lawns with the same flower beds and the same trophy cars parked outside the garages where everyone could see them, I came to a very different front lawn. It was bigger than most and had no flower beds. Instead, it had a variety of bushes and trees scattered around, all cut into elaborate designs. I saw a bear, a dove, an angel, a female figure, a shamrock, and some geometric shapes. A fresh bouquet of flowers leaned against the mailbox.

I passed the house and parked a little way down the street. A couple of people were strolling down the street in the opposite direction, but otherwise, no one was around.

Walking over to the lawn, I wondered which bush he had been working on when he came to his sticky end. Most likely, it was one of the ones that weren't finished yet. Some were trimmed and tidy, while others had some stray leaves and ends of branches sticking out, marring the fine contours. Poor Archibald had died halfway through spring trimming.

I went over to the bouquet. A card said "From the Cheerville Gardening Society. Rest in peace in the garden of paradise." I imagined the deceased trimming bushes in heaven. I suppose that would be paradise for him. Of course, James was in heaven too, and his idea of paradise was blowing things up alongside Latina guerrillas toting Kalashnikovs. He always did like those Latina guerillas a little too much. I wondered how those two visions of a perfect afterlife would work together. Would James blow up Archibald's bushes? That hardly seemed fair.

One of the unfinished bushes caught my eye. It was the shamrock, set by the side of the house between the wall and a high hedge that delineated his property from his neighbor's. One half of the design was neatly trimmed, while the other still needed a lot of work. I surveyed the other bushes and found all were either fully trimmed or not trimmed at all. Only the shamrock was halfway done.

Glancing around to make sure no one was looking, I walked across the lawn.

I'm no expert on topiary, but on closer inspection, it was obvious that part of the shamrock had been finished, and part was left to be done later. A prizewinning gardener would probably finish the job, not leave a bush half done.

Unless he never got the chance to finish it.

Something caught my eye behind the bush. I had to edge around the giant shamrock to get between it and the wall, and I found myself in a narrow space between the house and the boundary hedge. The earth was mostly bare since it didn't get much direct light, and the little grass that did grow in this hidden strip of ground was kicked up in places.

I saw several footprints from two different pairs of shoes. There was also a tray of flowers in little plastic boxes, just like the ones I'd bought. It was sitting at an odd angle, and some of the dirt had come out of it, as if it had been dropped, not set down. It didn't look like a place a prizewinning gardener would put a tray of flowers, anyway. I pulled out my phone and took some pictures.

Then I noticed the wall of the house. A big patch right behind the bush had recently been washed. It was cleaner than the rest of the wall. A long garden hose wound around a metal coil hanging on the wall a few feet away told me how it had been cleaned.

I examined the bush but didn't see any obvious place where the hedge clippers could have slipped, no half-cut branch with a knot in it that could have made the power tool spring back and hit the topiary expert in the neck. No, this wasn't an accident. And it didn't look like suicide either.

It looked like a murder someone was trying to cover up.

I was standing where Archibald had been

killed. There had been a struggle that had churned up the earth. Then the murderer killed him with his own hedge clippers before cleaning up the scene, getting rid of the spray of blood on the wall.

But why? Why get rid of the blood if you didn't get rid of the body?

I suspected whoever had killed him had been known to Archibald. That was playing the odds—most murders were committed by people known to the victim—but also common sense. Someone had lured Archibald to the one place he could be expected to be using his hedge clippers, but was also out of sight of the street and the neighbors, and then killed him.

Archibald had probably been holding the tray of flowers and dropped it immediately when he'd been attacked. I didn't see any bloodstains on the tray, but it could have been cleaned by the hose too. Perhaps that was when he'd been cut on the forehead. Then, before he could defend himself or even bring up his hands—since there was no mention of defensive wounds to the hands or arms—the murderer had cut him in the neck. Perhaps they'd fought over the hedge clippers, hence the disturbed soil. The murderer had been stronger than Archibald, not that that narrowed down the type of suspect much. Archibald may have been relatively fit, but he was in his eighties.

The murder scene told me something else too. Whoever had done it was an amateur. First off, they'd used a murder weapon that didn't jibe well with the suicide idea. Plus, while they had washed the wall, they hadn't obscured all the footprints. Whoever killed him had probably seen one of those cop shows talking about how blood trails can indicate angle of impact and all that, and worried the blood would suggest the cut had not been self-inflicted. That was debatable in any case, but an amateur might have felt concerned about such a thing.

Not covering up the footprints was "a n00b move," as my grandson would say. "N00b" was short for "newbie," as in "neophyte," a word I am certain has disappeared from the modern lexicon as much as the word "lexicon" has. Why "n00b" was spelled with two zeros was beyond me. Anyway, footprints were almost as good as fingerprints. A proper lab could tell quite a bit from a footprint.

I did not have a proper lab, however, and with my vision the way it was, I couldn't even study the footprints properly. I'd have to load the pictures onto my computer and enlarge them.

The footprints had already told me something,

however. Police Chief Grimal was not the murderer. He may have been an overdrinking small-town cop with an easy job, but he was no n00b. He was covering for someone else, not himself.

Taking some photos of the wall and shamrock, I moved along the side of the house but didn't see anything else interesting. The little alleyway led to a backyard. No topiary there, just some lawn furniture, a birdbath, and some flower beds.

I was just heading back the way I came, edging around the shamrock again, when disaster struck.

A car pulled up in front of the house. I ducked behind the shamrock and watched as a man and woman in their late forties or early fifties got out. They resembled each other, so I guessed they were related, not married. The fact that they both looked sad suggested they knew the victim.

Luckily, I'd parked my car fifty yards down the street and on the opposite side, a regular precaution so the subjects didn't suspect they were being watched. The pair walked up to the front door, and the woman produced a key and unlocked the door. *Two of Archibald's children?*

I caught a snatch of conversation.

"You going to deal with the bank today?" the woman asked.

"Yes." The man sighed. "Dad's finances are a

mess, though. I have to call the credit card companies and provide proof he's deceased."

"He really maxed out all of them?"

"Cash advances. Why didn't he tell us? We could have helped."

They closed the door behind them, and I heard no more.

I peeked out from behind the shamrock, feeling like a naughty leprechaun, and saw the front blinds were down. Hoping they didn't choose that moment to raise them, I hurried back to the sidewalk and strolled as calmly as I could back to my car.

I drove away deep in thought. I now had a motive—debt. If our dear departed topiary man had maxed out his credit cards to get cash advances, it meant he owed someone big time and had obviously not been able to pay enough for the murderer's satisfaction. Killing someone is a poor way to collect what you're owed, though. More likely, the real reason Archibald was killed was that he was being put under pressure to pay, couldn't manage it, and threatened to go to the police.

Drugs? Unlikely. Organized crime? Perhaps. North Korean agents had infiltrated the American Topiary Society, intent on stealing our lawn decorating secrets for their own nefarious purposes?

Well, that would certainly get me back in my comfort zone.

So I had a possible motive, but I still didn't have the reasons behind that motive, nor did I have a likely suspect. I knew almost nothing about the man and knew no one who knew him. The two ladies I'd eavesdropped on at the Cheerville Garden Centre seemed unlikely suspects, as did Archibald's children.

I only had a couple of other leads—his gardening society and his yoga classes. The murderer was most likely a member of one of those organizations.

So of course, I needed to join both of them.

THREE

The Cheerville Senior Center did not have an English theme and therefore had its "e" and its "r" in the proper order. It was a rambling one-story structure at the center of a spacious, well-mani-cured stretch of green bounded by woods. To one side stood a duck pond that glittered in the sunlight.

Several bushes had been shaped into topiaries of kittens and children. There was one impressive sculpture of a little girl holding a balloon, her dress swirling around her legs as if blowing in the wind. A slim branch served as the string of the balloon, a sphere of greenery making up the balloon itself.

Oak and birch trees provided shade for the various white-painted benches that were scattered here and there. Only a few were occupied even though the parking lot was nearly full. Cheerville's seniors weren't the outdoorsy type. They came to the senior center not for a chance to enjoy nature, but to socialize with other aged locals and engage in the various activities put on by the staff.

Or so I'd heard. I had never been to the Cheerville Senior Center or any other senior center. Like everyone else, I resented growing old, and I saw no need to be constantly reminded of it.

Clucking my tongue in disapproval, I took a couple of turns around the parking lot, finally found an empty space, and parked. Feeling conspicuous in my running shoes, T-shirt, and sweat pants, I passed through the sliding glass doors, which whooshed open at my approach—presumably so that my decrepit body wouldn't have to suffer the agonies of turning a doorknob—and entered the main lobby.

The temperature inside was perfect. Relaxing, mentally-unchallenging music played at a low volume through a hidden sound system. In one corner, a pair of Cheerville's elder generation snoozed on a pair of identical armchairs. Paintings of flowers and landscapes adorned the walls. I almost turned and ran.

Summoning my courage, I approached the main desk, where a young woman gave me an unconvincing smile, the kind of smile required in employee manuals. She was dressed all in white like a nurse, but without an actual nurse's uniform.

"Where is the yoga class being held?" I asked.

"Seniors Yoga is in the Jockey Room," she said in a voice a little louder than necessary. I suppose she thought I was deaf. "Just take that hallway all the way to the end. It's the last door on the right. It's already started."

Thanking her, I set off, already irritated. Why did they need to call it "Seniors Yoga"? It was held in a senior center, so wasn't that already obvious? Were they just trying to rub it in?

I walked down the well-carpeted hall with its soothing colors, soft music, and bland paintings. I never thought I'd miss Kabul until I saw this place.

Another young woman, dressed all in white like the one at the front desk, came out of a door and gave me a flat smile.

"Are you lost, honey?" she asked in a volume more suitable for calling me from the other end of the building.

"Are you trained to speak louder than normal?"

To her credit, she didn't skip a beat. "Yes, I am. Are you lost?"

"I'm going to Seniors Yoga."

"That's in the—"

"Jockey Room, last door on the right," I said, finishing her sentence.

Her grin got wider. "Very good!"

She walked down the hall toward the main entrance. She had said that like she was complimenting a three-year-old on his finger painting. Plus, she'd turned up the volume. Was she messing with me? Did she know I could break both her arms?

Well, these days, breaking both her arms would probably throw my back out and leave me bedridden for a week, but I could still do it.

Shaking my head, I went to the last door on the right, which was adorned with a brass sign that said Jockey Room in large, easy-to-read letters.

I had been wondering why it was called the Jockey Room, and now I got the answer.

Remember lawn jockeys? They were these little metal statues of black boys dressed up as jockeys. They had red caps and vests, white pants, and shiny black boots, and they held a lamp. People put them on their front lawns. Most weren't caricatures, the faces looked natural, but they did seem out of place on the lawns of wealthy white families who knew no black people other than their servants.

The story goes that they were made in honor of Jocko, George Washington's nine-year-old stable boy who volunteered to hold the general's horse during a storm one cold winter night. The general returned the next morning to find the boy frozen stiff, his hands still clasping the reins. To commemorate this show of loyalty, Washington was said to have made the first lawn jockey to adorn his front lawn at Mount Vernon. I have no idea if that was true, and I never really understood the point of lawn jockeys. It was just one of those odd things rich people did.

I don't know if the NAACP ever had a concerted campaign to get rid of lawn jockeys, or if Jesse Jackson ever led any protest marches through rich, white neighborhoods to make the residents throw out those bizarre and vaguely offensive lawn ornaments. I'm not sure the NAACP and Mr. Jackson even cared. They had enough on their plate as it was.

In any case, during the eighties, the lawn jockeys started to disappear. By some unspoken agreement, people decided they were racist, and people didn't want to be perceived as racist, least of all the racists themselves. Some lawn jockeys were given a coat of white paint on their faces in an attempt to make them socially acceptable, but that only made them more hideous, and even those soon began to disappear. By the end of the decade, you could hardly find a single one. A staple of suburban America had vanished, replaced by the equally grotesque but politically neutral garden gnome. I had always wondered what happened to the old-fashioned lawn jockey.

Now I knew. The lawn jockeys had all come to the Cheerville Senior Center.

They lined all four walls. There must have been almost a hundred of them, a diminutive army of outmoded political incorrectness. Some still had their covering of white paint, that last-ditch effort to make them socially acceptable, while on others, the white paint had started flaking off. Most, however, had their original black faces. They all stood facing inwards, holding out their lanterns as if to illuminate the Seniors Yoga class going on within their smiling circle.

The yoga class looked as out of fashion as the lawn jockeys. Three tidy rows of Cheerville's senior citizens stood on yoga mats, their legs planted at shoulder width and their hands raised in the air. The array of pink and yellow sweat pants was almost blinding. A healthy-looking woman in her forties stood in front. She was obviously the instructor. She was the only one who fit properly into her stretch pants.

There seemed to be some sort of hierarchy in

the class. The oldest all stood in the front row, perhaps so if they toppled over, the teacher could catch them. The younger ladies stood in the second row. The back row had only a few guys.

I was wondering why all the guys were in the back row until the teacher called out, "Forward fold!" and everyone bent forward. Or tried to bend forward. Some almost touched their toes. Others just sort of leaned a little. The men barely bent over at all. They were too busy staring at all the behinds pushed out in front of them.

Boys will be boys, even when they're old men.

"Aaaand, stretch!"

Everyone inhaled and stood up straight, or as straight as they could. Withered arms and arthritic fingers reached for the ceiling. The faces looked serene. I'd heard yoga was good for meditation, and it certainly seemed like it was wiping these ladies' cares away. The guys in the back row were getting some psychological benefit too.

"Hello!" The yoga instructor greeted me in a chirpy voice. To her credit, she actually said this in a normal volume. "Take your shoes off and join us. There's a spare yoga mat in the back row if you don't mind sharing space with the guys."

I didn't mind at all. If I was in the back row,

they wouldn't be ogling me every time I made a yoga move.

Slipping off my sneakers, I took my place just in time to do another forward fold. Hip joints snapped and male eyeballs popped all across the room.

"Aaaand, stretch!" the instructor called again.

We stretched.

Then came something called Warrior Pose, where you bend the front leg, stretch out the back leg, and put your body sideways while stretching out your arms horizontally. I'm not sure why it was called Warrior Pose, since it didn't seem like a good pose for shooting or stabbing someone, but it was a decent way to stretch. Looking around the room, it appeared I was the only warrior in the crowd, except for a couple of men who looked like veterans of the Napoleonic Wars.

Not all of the men in the room were aging perverts. The man next to me looked remarkably fit. Young too. He didn't look a day over 65, although I guessed he was probably a bit older if he was hanging out with this crowd. He wasn't even looking at the row of bottoms arrayed before him.

He was looking at me.

And smiling.

"You're new, aren't you?" he asked.

"None of us are new," I replied.

He flashed me a grin, showing a good set of teeth that were flawed just enough to convince me they were real. His hair was real too, and he had a full head of it. It was mostly gray, but I had long since stopped being picky about such things.

"I'm Octavian," he said. The last syllable came out somewhat strained as we did something called Tree Pose, which involved getting on one leg and resting the foot of the other below the knee. He nearly pitched over right into me. I got the feeling he wouldn't have minded that at all.

"After the Roman emperor?" I asked.

"My father was a Classics professor."

"I'm Barbara. Pleased to meet you."

"I'm glad to hear that," he said. The way he said it made me feel something I hadn't felt in quite a long time. I tamped it down. I had a murder to investigate. I also had to maintain Tree Pose, which was more difficult than it should have been. I tried to remember the last time I had stood on one leg and couldn't recall.

Of course, I was doing better than everyone else in the room except for the instructor. There had already been several stumbles, and a few of the students weren't even trying. They just stood there, which was probably wise on their part.

The instructor grew serious, her features darkening from her previous calm.

"Now, it's time for meditation. All of you lie down on your yoga mats with your arms and legs spread slightly apart. Try to clear your mind and let your muscles relax. I know we're all thinking about poor Archibald—"

At this point Octavian made a little grunting noise, like he'd been punched in the stomach.

"So perhaps we could send good thoughts through the cosmos to that happy place where his consciousness now resides."

Everyone lay down on their mats. I followed suit, trying not to think about how many stinky septuagenarian socks had rubbed against its rubbery surface. I was hoping the instructor would say more about Archibald, but she only stood there looking sad. I glanced at Octavian. He looked pretty grim too. He took a deep breath, exhaled slowly, and closed his eyes.

Everyone else did the same, so I figured that was what I was supposed to do. This was the first time I had been to a yoga class. Karate and pistol practice were more my thing.

In fact, the meditation turned out to be quite relaxing. Even though I had come late to class and had only done a few minutes of stretching and exercise, lying down on a springy yoga mat with a soft carpet beneath it, breathing deeply and slowly, in and out, in a quiet room, quickly put me at ease. With my eyes closed, I could even ignore the grinning stares of the lawn jockeys, which, I have to admit, made me a bit self-conscious.

Yes, it was relaxing. So relaxing that one of the guys to my left started snoring.

I opened my eyes and peeked, only to see Octavian looking at me.

We both looked away then glanced back at each other. Octavian jerked his head in the direction of the snorer and flashed me another grin. I smiled back.

Hmm, perhaps this wasn't part of the class. I made a point of looking back at the ceiling and closing my eyes.

We lay like that for several minutes, but I was no longer relaxed. I was wondering if Octavian was still staring at me. It had been a long time since I'd attracted that much attention from a man who wasn't trying to kill me.

You don't know that for sure yet, I reminded myself. *You're on a murder investigation, remember, and right now, pretty much anyone who knew the victim is a suspect.*

When the instructor announced our meditation period was over and we could all get up and go, I smiled at Octavian and stepped over to talk with him.

Just for the sake of the investigation, of course.

"Are you a gardener?" I asked. I figured that would be a good question to ask someone who had known Archibald without it sounding like a pickup line. I didn't want this gentleman to get the wrong idea.

Octavian cocked his head and gave me a smile. "You know, no one has ever accused me of that before. The closest thing to gardening I ever did was mowing the lawn when I was a kid."

"Oh, I just figured, since you knew Archibald…"

He stiffened. "Um, no. We were just friends. Did you know him from one of his gardening clubs?"

"No. I'm fairly new to town, and I'm just getting into gardening. Everyone kept telling me to talk to him because he was such a local talent. I heard he even won awards."

Octavian rolled up his yoga mat and nodded. "He sure did. Pity you never got to meet him. A good man. Care for a drink?"

The sudden change in subject was accompanied by a piercing gaze that made me feel put on the spot, although in a good way.

"Um, sure," I said.

A "drink," fortunately, didn't involve going to some dive bar. My dive bar days are, thankfully, long over. Too many fights. Have you ever had a beer bottle broken over your head? It's not a pleasant experience, I can tell you. Thank God I'd had my hair tied up in a bun. Otherwise, I would have needed surgery rather than just stitches.

No, Octavian wasn't the dive bar type, at least not on a first date, and he sure was acting like it was a date. This guy worked fast. He even paid for my strawberry apple smoothie at the senior center's snack bar like he'd just ordered a two-hundred-dollar bottle of champagne.

We made the usual small talk for the first few minutes. Octavian had moved to Cheerville when he retired, just like I had. He'd worked as a stockbroker in the city for most of his professional career and had grown tired of city life, so Cheerville was the obvious choice, once he no longer needed to be in the city for work. He did let drop that he missed some of the excitement, although you could "find some excitement locally." This led to the casual mention that he was a widower, at which point I casually mentioned I was a widow. Just to keep the conversation on an equal basis, of course.

Then the conversation took a sudden turn.

"Do you like horses?" he asked. "Every little girl likes horses."

I laughed. "I haven't been a little girl in a long, long time."

"Ah, but you're young at heart. I can tell. Do you follow the Grand National?"

I was vaguely aware that the Grand National was England's biggest horse race and that it was coming up soon. I decided to fake an interest.

"Oh, those horses are so beautiful! I don't know much about the races, but they're always fascinating to watch."

At this point, Octavian launched into a lecture about horse racing. Men love to show off their knowledge. Younger women call this "mansplaining" and cry sexism, but men do it to each other too. It's not so much sexism as it is the modern version of primal chest thumping. I've noticed the amount of mansplaining is generally in inverse proportion to the amount of actual chest thumping the man in question gets to do. Dear old James, with his detonators and Third World insurgencies, hardly ever mansplained.

Octavian had obviously never blown up a bridge or taken down a rogue government, because he mansplained quite a bit. At least he knew what he was talking about, unlike some of the guys at the shooting range. I loved enduring a lecture about firearms from some show-off half my age and then placing eight rounds in a tight cluster at the center of the target from fifty yards. The guy's jaw would drop like he'd just tried to swallow a bowling ball.

But I knew next to nothing about horses, so I nodded and made interested noises as Octavian taught me far more than I ever wanted to know. In the back of my mind, a little bell was going off. Horse racing meant betting, and betting meant debts. From the snippet of conversation I'd over-heard, Archibald Heaney had a large amount of debt.

"So which horse should I back?" I interjected.

Octavian's eyes lit up. "Ah! I'd pick Kentucky Pride for first place and Ghost of a Chance for second."

"Ghost of a Chance? That's not a name that inspires confidence."

"Oh, he's a sure one to place." This set off a lecture about why his two picks were clear winners, even though the odds were against them. Most of his reasoning was spurious, based not on the horses' past performances, but on some complex relation-ship between which horse had been in which races and at what starting gate. It all sounded like numerology to me.

I got a sinking feeling in my stomach. Octavian was going down in my estimation. You didn't need to be a mathematical genius to know gambling was a fool's game with the odds stacked against you. So many people fell into it, though, chasing some imagined streak of luck rather than rationally thinking about what they were doing. Octavian seemed like a nice man, so it bothered me to see that feverish gleam in his eye. I didn't really want to think about why that bothered me so much.

That little bell in the back of my mind was ringing louder now. Betting on horse races was illegal in our state and every neighboring state. Octavian, however, was definitely betting on the races. So where was he doing it?

I knew how to find out.

I looked around as if to be sure no one was listening, leaned forward conspiratorially, "unconsciously" moved my hand closer to his, and looked him in the eye as I smiled.

"So where would a lady find a place to have some fun with the horses in this dull little town?"

FOUR

It didn't look like much from the outside, just a plain shop front in a strip mall at the edge of town, set between a hardware store and an electronics outlet. A nondescript sign said Cheerville Social Club. A notice on the door said Members Only. The windows were shaded.

"Don't worry about that," Octavian said, gesturing at the sign. "As a longtime member, I can vouch for you."

The background check the club ran on me would vouch for me too. When Octavian took my number after our little smoothie date at the senior center, he was quite particular about getting my full name. He'd also asked enough questions to know when I had come to Cheerville, where I had lived before that, and even my birthday. Not that he asked me how old I was—he was too much of a gentleman—but he did get the date of my birthday out of me.

I know when I'm being interrogated. Enough secret agents have tried to do it to me that I have a sixth sense about such things, and those secret agents were far better at it than Octavian. Not that he was clumsy or obvious. If not for my training, I would have never noticed our two-hour-long conversation—yes, we took that much time over our smoothies—had been peppered with various questions that, when strung together, made a good profile of yours truly that pinpointed me among all the other Barbara Golds in the world. This "social club" wanted to make sure I wasn't a cop or a reporter or even worse, some sort of self-appointed social campaigner.

The fact that Octavian went to such pains to check on me indicated this was an organized operation. I suspected he had passed on the information to whoever ran this place for more detailed checks. This probably happened with all new members. Since I was here, it looked like I had passed muster.

As Octavian knocked, I noticed a small security camera placed unobtrusively above the door.

The door opened. A large young man who

looked like he weighed about two hundred fifty pounds, all of it muscle, stood on the other side. Beyond him was a tiny front room with another door on the opposite wall.

"Good afternoon, Mr. Perry," the guard said. This was not a doorman, I could tell. This was a guard.

"Good afternoon, Lance," Octavian said. "This is the guest I told you about."

Lance gave the semblance of a bow. "You are most welcome, Mrs. Gold."

I disliked Lance immediately. He had a reptilian look in his eyes. I'd seen that look in gangsters and hardcore thugs many a time. Not all gangsters and thugs, mind you. Most criminals were lost or lazy people who had gotten sidetracked from an honest life because of one thing or another. While they deserved to be punished, there was still some humanity in them. They could be turned around. Not so with people who looked at you like they were a lizard, and you were a big, juicy fly.

How could someone as nice as Octavian get mixed up with someone like this guy?

Gambling, that was how. It was an addiction for some people, and addicts don't get picky about the company they keep.

My senses kicked into overdrive, taking in every

move the doorman made. My exterior, however, remained calm. To everyone who saw me, I was a sweet little old lady with no combat training whatsoever. I didn't look like a threat to anyone.

Actually, since I had left my gun at home, I wasn't really much of a threat anyway, certainly not to a man-mountain like Lance.

Lance closed the door to the outside, slid a dead bolt across it with an ominous air, then opened the interior door and turned to Octavian.

"Guests have to pay a cover charge, sir."

The gangster tried to sound polite but failed. Courtesy wasn't part of his manner.

"Ah, yes." Octavian slipped him a fifty-dollar bill. I tried to object, but he waved my concerns aside. "My treat. It's rare I have such nice company."

We entered, my body stiffening at having to turn my back on the doorman. Octavian seemed oblivious. I could see his eyes lighting up with that eager gleam people get when they are about to get a fix of their drug of choice.

The inside of Cheerville's secret gambling den was, I must admit, a bit of a letdown. I was hoping a grand casino was hidden behind this bland façade, with croupiers in tuxedos, slinky supermodels pickpocketing millionaire gamblers, and perhaps an opium den in the back just for chuckles.

No such luck. Cheerville was dull even when it was being illicit. What I saw was an interior about the size of a medium-sized store, all one room except for a closed door on the far wall that must have led to a back room, judging from the depth of the strip mall compared to the room I was standing in. A dozen tables were scattered here and there, most of them occupied. There was a croupier, but he wasn't in a tuxedo. He was a muscular guy in jeans and a T-shirt, running a roulette wheel for a few men and women who were placing their bets. As the staccato *click click click* of the ball going around the wheel echoed across the room, I looked at the other tables. Most were occupied by people staring at one of a number of TVs on the wall, showing horse and greyhound races. Despite it being before noon, some had beer or mixed drinks in front of them, courtesy of a small wet bar tucked in one corner, manned by another reptilian.

Senior citizens made up the majority of the members. That didn't surprise me, considering it was the middle of a workday. I'd have to get Octavian to bring me back at night to see what kind of crowd showed up then.

Octavian hooked an arm around mine. As

much as I disliked the side of him I was seeing at the moment, I couldn't help but feel a slight quickening of the pulse. Purely due to the hazardous situation we were in, of course.

"What do you think?" he asked.

"Certainly more interesting than the senior center," I conceded.

We found an empty table and sat down.

"Would you like a drink?" he asked.

"Does he make smoothies?" I asked. I'd never been much of a drinker, and I never drank on the job.

Octavian laughed. The reptile from behind the bar came over.

"An orange juice for me," Octavian said, his respectability nudging up slightly in my estimation. I've never liked daytime drinkers. "And anything the lady likes."

"An orange juice would be fine, thanks."

The bartender nodded and walked off without a word. Octavian pulled a racing magazine out of his pocket and began to explain it to me. There were a bewildering number of races across several countries, and the TVs here caught all the major ones. I listened and nodded to his lecture as I glanced around me. The bartender came back with our drinks and two racing forms.

"Greyhounds or horses?" Octavian asked.

"Horses, I think."

"I prefer those too. Poor old Archibald preferred greyhounds. He had no luck with them, though."

Bingo.

"Oh, that's too bad," I said. "Did he lose a lot?"

Octavian winced and shrugged. "Yes, unfortunately he did. He didn't know when to stop. Look, there's a race coming up in Mexico we can do. Now, I know a bit about the Mexican thoroughbreds…"

I decided not to ask more questions about Archibald immediately. That might raise suspicions. I'd already confirmed my main supposition— Archibald was a gambler and lost a lot of money. That was why he maxed out his credit cards. Had he lost enough that he had to borrow from the heavies who ran this place? Would that be enough to get him killed? I'd have to learn more.

Of course, I already had enough to go to Police Chief Grimal. This was an illegal gambling parlor operating within the city limits. If he raided it, he could arrest the operators and pump them for information about Archibald's death.

Except I couldn't trust him. Grimal had ruled Archibald's death hadn't been suspicious, even though it so obviously was. Without seeing the autopsy report, I couldn't tell if the county coroner had made that decision as well or had been over-ruled by Grimal. My bet was that they both decided Archibald had magically cut his own throat with hedge clippers. But why? Were they trying to protect the murderer?

At least I could cross off Octavian as a suspect. If he had killed Archibald, he would have never revealed this place to me. I've never liked it when murderers flirted with me, and I felt glad that wasn't happening now.

And flirting he was. If that smoothie at the senior center had been like a champagne breakfast, he acted like taking me out gambling was the equivalent of going on a whirlwind tour of the Caribbean. He kept gazing into my eyes and leaning in close, making little jokes or flattering comments. Octavian must have been a lady killer when he was younger.

In the lulls in conversation when we watched the races—in other words, watched our horses lose time and again—I considered what I felt about all this. You can't reach the age of seventy in a dangerous and demanding career without having a bit of personal insight into your own nature. I knew I was relishing the attention.

For many years, James was all that I needed. There had been no other men after we got serious, and while there had been plenty of offers over the years, I had never been seriously tempted. James never cheated either, despite all those missions with Latina guerrillas. I checked. Oh yes, I checked, and it's a good thing for him that he didn't fall into temptation. We remained enough for each other emotionally and physically. By the time James died, I was of an age where those physical things didn't really matter all that much anymore, so I sort of put it out of my mind. I still noticed a handsome man if I passed one in the street, and I still enjoyed any little compliment or second glance that came my way.

Unfortunately, those compliments and glances had become increasingly rare in recent years, so Octavian's attention came as a pleasant and unexpected surprise.

But how did this make me feel about James's memory? I did, of course, sense a twinge of guilt. We had always told each other that if one died before the other instead of dying together in some massive explosion, the other should move on with their life. Easy to say, not so easy to do.

I comforted myself with the knowledge that, at the age of seventy, I wasn't about to get swept up in a torrid love affair that would rival anything James and I had enjoyed. It had been quite the whirlwind in the early years, before settling down into a deep and trusting companionship that maintained the physical aspect long after many couples have departed for separate bedrooms.

So Octavian wasn't about to sweep me off my feet. I'd enjoy the attention while honoring James's memory. And why not? James was probably looking down from heaven with a wry smile, glad I was getting out and not turning into a crazy cat lady.

I could also justify this because I was on a mission. James certainly owed me plenty on that score. More than once, he had to share a tent with those Latina guerrillas because they had to "travel light." On some covert ops, he even shared hotel rooms with women while posing as a married couple. I always arranged to go to the shooting range with the woman in question before the mission started in order to show her what I was capable of if she descended into method acting.

Just as I thought this, the mission got a whole lot more interesting. I noticed one of the heavies was pushing the tables together.

"What's going on?" I asked.

"Lunchtime."

"They have a restaurant here?"

Octavian chuckled. "No, but they bring around a bunch of takeout menus and fetch it for us. That way we don't miss any of the races."

"Great idea! Let's stay for lunch." *Yes, let's sit at a big table with a bunch of murder suspects.*

One of the workers passed out menus for half a dozen local restaurants that offered takeout. We picked Thai. I'd always liked spicy food, and so, I found, did Octavian. I might have needed reading glasses to see the sights on my 9mm, I might not walk as quickly as I used to, and my knees and back might trouble me, but I still had an iron stomach. After all the food poisoning, parasites, and diseases I'd picked up from eating local cuisine in various jungles, deserts, and slums, no Five Alarm Special from a Thai restaurant in a rich American town was going to phase me.

As we waited for our food, we watched a couple more races and even managed to win one. You wouldn't have known that race was the one bright spot in our losing streak by the way Octavian acted. His face lit up, and he pumped his fist in the air like some teenager who had just scored a touchdown for his high school football team.

I was now only fifty dollars poorer than when I had come in. Octavian had been betting more and was down two hundred and forty dollars. Yes, I was keeping track.

The food came, and everyone gathered around to eat and trade anecdotes about the morning's luck. Octavian became his chatty best and introduced me to all of them. His arm slipped around my shoulders as he did so. Some of the older men looked on with envy. Octavian had a way with people. He certainly had a way with me.

A few hardcore members ate in silence, placing bets with the bookies who ran this place and watching races throughout their meal. The bookies must have been making a mint. I doubted any of these obsessives had bumped off poor Archibald. I was going on the assumption that he had been killed because he owed someone money, and I doubted the hardcore gamblers would, or even could, have lent him any.

I turned to the other candidates in our little circle, scratching off a few people as too old or physically infirm. I also scratched off one middle-aged man who proclaimed he'd just returned from seeing his parents in Florida and had come directly to the club. He pointed to his suitcase by the door as if this was something to show off. "I haven't even seen the wife yet," he said with obvious pride. Much as I would have liked to get that idiot in trouble, he was obviously not the murderer.

That left only a few suspects.

Tim Harding was a quiet man in his fifties who owned some apartment buildings in town. He was tall and lanky, with big hands and feet, and a crew cut that hinted he'd been in the army some years ago. I had actually met him before, although I don't think he remembered me. When I first moved into town, I rented an apartment in one of his buildings for a couple of months as my new house got renovated. He was active in municipal and county politics and tried to get me to join various organizations. I politely declined. I had been active in a very different brand of politics, and I'd come to Cheerville to relax. One detail I recalled was how proud he was of the topiary around the pool of the apartment complex. I'd admired the bushes myself as my grandson splashed around in the pool. The boy had been deeply disappointed when I moved into my house and lost access to a free place to swim.

The connection to topiary was interesting, but Tim spoke so little over lunch I couldn't get anything else out of him.

Cynthia McAlister I pegged as a bored housewife. She was in her thirties and already going to seed, overweight with poor table manners and dressed in a sloppy fashion. She didn't seem to care and didn't make much of an effort to talk to me. All through the meal, she kept looking over at the roulette wheel and shaking her head. I remembered she had spent most of the past two hours there.

"Lose a lot, Cynthia?" Octavian asked.

"Yeah," she sighed in a tone that made me think that was normal for her.

"This place is rigged, I tell you."

This came from George Whitaker. The man scowled all through lunch, griping about how much money he had lost. He was an accountant in his late thirties, taking a break from his private business to gamble half the workday away.

"Oh, you're just having a bad streak. It'll turn around," Octavian said.

"No, damn it!" George said, hitting the table with his fist. He quickly looked around to make sure none of the staff had heard then continued in a low voice. "That roulette wheel hardly ever pays out, and I've missed five races in a row, and some of those dogs were sure things."

Octavian nodded his head toward Tim. "He's won the roulette several times. Didn't you win six hundred dollars last week, Tim?"

Tim smiled and gave a humble shrug.

"Some people have all the luck," Cynthia sighed.

"And in any case, they couldn't have fixed the races," I said, wondering how anyone could be so stupid as to think betting on a race could be a "sure thing".

"They're all in it together," George scoffed.

I resisted the urge to roll my eyes. Luckily, at this point, someone far more pleasant started to chat me up.

Ricardo Morales was a rarity in Cheerville— someone who wasn't white. Cheerville was one of the whitest towns I'd ever seen, with few residents who were minorities. The lawn jockeys in the senior center didn't count.

Ricardo was born in Mexico City and legally immigrated to the United States when he was a young man on the strength of a degree in engineering. My antenna went up at that, and I casually asked where he worked. "So kind of you to assume I'm still of working age," he said, nodding his lovely head with its salt and pepper hair. "I retired last year from Boeing."

That got my interest. Archibald had worked at Boeing. They had a big plant not far from Cheerville.

Ricardo chatted with me the most, politely

asking me what I thought of Cheerville and putting on the charm. Octavian started to get a little jealous, which I thought was amusing, and tried to steer the conversation to other people.

Ricardo steered it right back by raising a glass of wine and proposing a toast.

"To Archibald."

"He was a good man," Octavian sighed.

George nodded. Tim's eyes filled, and I saw those big hands tremble a little. Cynthia's gaze shifted back to the roulette wheel.

Everyone raised their glasses and drank.

"I heard you're giving the speech at the memorial service," Octavian said.

"It will be an honor," Ricardo said, bowing his head.

The conversation lapsed.

"I can't believe he killed himself," Cynthia said in a way that showed she did believe it, but it surprised her.

"This damn place drove him to it," George griped.

I glanced around the table. Everyone looked sad, except for George, who looked like he wanted to launch into an angry speech but controlled himself out of consideration for the situation.

"Not just this place," Ivan Dejevsky said. He

was a balding man with an impressive paunch. I pegged him to be in his sixties and not well preserved. Octavian had introduced me to him, but this was the first thing he'd said since.

Ivan and George looked significantly at another man sitting alone at a table some distance away, watching the races. He had a smug look on his face and was well dressed, although that didn't hide his bald spot and a paunch to rival Ivan's.

No one seemed about to say anything, so I took a chance.

"Who is that?" I asked.

"Gary Milner. He's an ace with the horses," Octavian said with obvious respect. "The best I've ever seen. He'll lend you money if you're hard up."

"Lend *some* people money," Ivan griped.

"Yeah, some people get preferential treatment with that guy," George said to me, "and some people are left out in the cold."

"Archibald was a good man," Tim said with an irritated tone. "An expert with topiary."

"I suppose," George said with a shrug. "I have better things to do than fiddle around with plants."

The conversation lapsed into a grim silence. I didn't want to push my luck by breaking it. I'd been given plenty to mull over.

When the conversation resumed again, it was

about the races. Nothing kept them off that subject for long.

So I finally had a tentative list of suspects: Tim the topiary fan, Cynthia the depressed loser, George the angry loser, Ricardo the former coworker, Ivan the champion of gamblers' rights, and Gary the stingy moneylender.

But why would one of them kill Archibald Heaney? Or could it be someone else entirely, someone I hadn't met yet? I needed to get to know these people better. That memorial service sounded like an excellent idea. I'd have to get myself invited somehow.

Of course, these weren't the only people who could have killed Archibald. Not all the club members were here, and it might not even be a club member. This was only a good place to start. The Cheerville Gardening Society would have to be my next stop. That was the other likely spot to find suspects. If it turned out any of the gamblers were also in that group, that would be a good lead. So far, only Tim might fit the bill on that score.

I did, however, think the criminals who ran this outfit weren't the ones who killed Archibald. They looked like pros to me. They wouldn't kill him over a debt because then they'd never get their money, plus they wouldn't have murdered him outside where they could have been spotted. Of course, they might have wanted to send a message, perhaps to strike fear into the heart of someone who owed them significantly more money, but they could have done that more safely simply by threatening the actual target.

No, the murder had been the work of an amateur, and I might very well be having lunch with the amateur in question.

Lunch ended all too soon, and the circle quickly broke up. Within minutes, everyone was staring at the screens again, lost in their little worlds of luck and hope. We gambled for a while longer, winning some and losing some but not regaining any of what we had already lost.

I hoped to get a chance to talk to the others again, but they remained at their own tables, encased in their own fantasies of easy wealth. It didn't look like I was going to get any more done today, and glancing at my watch, I decided it was getting time for me to leave anyway.

"I have to be at my son's house in an hour, and I need to swing by and feed the cat first," I told my date. It came out sounding like I had a curfew.

"Oh, that's too bad," he said. He looked longingly at the screens and at his racing form, torn between staying here or being the gentleman and leaving with me. I'm happy to say his gentlemanly side won.

"Did you have a good time?" Octavian asked as he walked me out.

"Yes," I said in all honesty.

"Great!" he said with a smile. "I was worried you might be turned off by losing."

"Oh well, it was educational."

Yes, very educational, but I still hadn't learned all I wanted to know. I needed to go back after hours and take a look around when no one was there.

But what I didn't know was that I had another mission to accomplish, and this one would be just as tricky.

FIVE

My son, Frederick, lived in an attractive New-England-style house in a good neighborhood in Cheerville. It stood at the end of a quiet cul-de-sac. Well, it would have been quiet if my grandson, Martin, wasn't practicing his mountain bike moves in the front yard.

He'd scrounged some plywood from Frederick's latest home-improvement project and propped them up on two tree stumps standing about twenty feet apart. He pedaled as fast as he could at one of the ramps, hit it with a loud bang, ricocheted off of it, wagging his front wheel in a way that was meant to look cool, thumped down on the grass, and pedaled for the other ramp, repeating the move with an even louder thump.

I could hear the noise from half a block away with the windows in my car rolled up. I couldn't imagine what the neighbors were thinking.

They were probably thinking Frederick had sent my grandson out there to drive them all away. Frederick was the town's leading real estate agent and made a tidy profit any time a house went up for sale.

I pulled into the driveway, honking to alert Martin just in case he decided to suddenly change direction and cross my path without looking. He responded by banking off a ramp, letting go of the handlebars, and waving with both hands. He barely gripped the handlebars in time to avoid crashing.

Thirteen-year-olds are immortal, you see. I often felt that if the CIA really wanted operatives who were fearless, they should hire teenagers.

Even though Martin saved himself from face-planting into the lawn, which was looking distinctly shredded from all his toing and froing, he didn't regain enough control of his bike to hit the ramp correctly. Instead of hitting the center of the board where it was supported by the tree, he hit the edge. He barreled straight through it, the board whipping around like a door being slammed, crashing into his back wheel.

Martin, already wobbly from showing off for his

grandmother, lost complete control of the bike and tumbled off, rolling to one side as the bike ploughed through a rose bush and lodged itself into my son's white picket fence.

I emerged from my car, applauding. I suppose I should have felt guilty considering it was indirectly my fault he fell, but I relished the attention almost as much as he did. For the longest time, I'd been the boring old fart who could safely be ignored in favor of video games. Thanks to a newly discovered mutual love of reading, I'd become Grandma once more. It was like he was six again, except more gratifying because the affection wasn't automatic.

Martin staggered to his feet, brushing his unruly blonde hair from his eyes. Nothing seemed broken or bleeding. Airplane pilots say any landing you walk away from is a good landing. I wondered if Martin would become an airline pilot. I'd develop a phobia of flying in that case.

"Did you bring Dandelion?" he asked as he walked over to his bike.

"No, she'd scratch my car's upholstery to bits! She's quite destructive for a kitten."

"She's not destructive," Martin said, stomping through the rose bush and yanking the bike out from where its front tire was stuck between two boards of the fence. One of the boards came with it.

Martin looked at me ruefully. "Don't tell Dad about that."

"My lips are sealed. Try to fix it."

He set the board against the fence and kicked it a couple of times. One of the nails sticking out of the board caught on another board and lodged in it. Despite it being at a forty-five-degree angle, Martin decided it looked convincing enough to fool his dad and got back on his bike, smashing more roses as he turned in a tight circle and cycled over to me.

"Finished the book yet?" he asked.

The book in question was *Dragon's Fire Book Four: Dragon's Hoard*, part of a young adult fantasy series Martin was devouring. It was nice to see him devour something other than burgers and his parents' property value. I'd already read books one through three. Martin was on book six.

"I'm halfway through," I told him. "They've just figured out how to cast a spell to move the rock in front of the cave."

Martin's eyes widened. "Then you're coming to the best part. They go in and—"

"No spoilers!"

"Oh, right."

We both laughed. I'm a "no spoilers" kind of girl. I don't even watch previews of movies I know I'm going to see, or read the blurbs of the latest books from my favorite authors.

"But it's good," I said. "I'm enjoying it as much as the first three."

Actually, I was enjoying being able to bond with my grandson. The books weren't bad, though. They were simple adventure fare following three teenagers who had to rid the world of dragons while dealing with typical teen problems.

The little wizard boy struggled with a crippling shyness but felt comfortable with his two companions. The warrior boy's family got killed in a dragon attack, and he was all alone in the world. He was the most undisciplined of the three and obviously needed a father figure, which he was slowly finding in the old sage who taught the adventurous trio dragon lore. The warrior girl, Skara, my favorite character, had to deal with the unwelcome attentions of a pervy uncle, who she put in his place time and again. He was the local lord, however, so Skara couldn't get him locked up. But she did manage to thwart his evil plans and was slowly undermining his position. I sensed the uncle would get a splendid comeuppance before the series ended. Young adult books were certainly more serious now than the ones I was raised on.

The front door opened, and my son, Frederick, appeared. Frederick, as much as I loved him, was not a chip off the old block. The apple had fallen very far from the tree. Any number of clichés could be used to describe just how different he was from me and his father.

First off, he had never heard a shot fired in anger. Frederick didn't even like war films or the violent video games Martin loved as much as his fantasy novels. He also didn't take care of himself. Despite being barely into middle age, he was developing quite the belly. His idea of exercise was taking clients around a home he was trying to sell.

He was a fine man, though, a warm spirit who loved his child so much that he pretended not to notice the broken fence.

Of course he noticed it immediately. It was his job to spot every detail of a piece of property, and the squashed rose bush and the crooked fence post weren't exactly inconspicuous.

"Hi, Mom!" he called to me with a friendly wave, his voice somewhat strained as he gave the fence a sidelong glance. "Martin, come on in. It's time for dinner."

As his father turned back inside, Martin gave

me a conspiratorial grin and a thumbs-up. He dumped his bike on the lawn and hurried inside. I followed him, chuckling and shaking my head. At times, I felt Frederick and Alicia were too soft on Martin. He got away with so much, and his room was a disaster area, but on the other hand, he was a sweet boy who got good grades and never got into any real trouble at school.

As I came inside, nearly tripping over Martin's skateboard and wending my way around a pair of just-discarded sneakers, I smelled the rich aroma of my daughter-in-law's famous lasagna. It wasn't famous for being particularly delicious, not that I can judge anyone's cooking, but because it was truly famous. It made it onto the front page of the *Cheerville Gazette* last year when she was making some and got so involved with a complex mathematical problem that she forgot she was cooking at all. A ringing smoke alarm, two fire trucks, and several hundred gallons of water later, she made it onto the front page under the banner headline Famed Local Physicist Creates Dark Matter in Oven. They even had a photo of what remained of the lasagna, and it did indeed look like the contents of a black hole.

Frederick had pulled his advertising from the paper for a month after that until he got an apology from both the editor and the reporter. Personally, I thought it was hilarious. The *Cheerville Gazette* was usually so boring.

I walked into the kitchen, both to check on the lasagna and to say hello to my daughter-in-law. Sadly, she was a rare sight around these parts. She was a noted particle physicist, working on some esoteric research project with the CERN reactor beneath the border of France and Switzerland. Half the time she was over there, and much of the rest of her time she was flying to various conferences. This year alone she'd been to the Imperial College in London, the European Southern Observatory in Chile, the Max Planck Institute in Germany, and so many stateside conferences that I'd lost track. Was it any wonder she sometimes forgot she had something in the oven? She was headed for a Nobel Prize or a heart attack. I wasn't sure which. Perhaps both.

Alicia was a thin, preoccupied-looking woman with long blond hair and a pretty face. She was most certainly not the stereotypical nerdy scientist type. She dressed in the latest fashions when she cared to and was conversant in art and literature as well as physics, astronomy, and the kind of mathematics we mere mortals couldn't ever hope to fathom.

When Frederick landed this prize catch, I knew James and I had raised him right. Many men couldn't handle a successful woman who was more intelligent than they were. Not so with Frederick. He adored her. The only friction I detected in their marriage was that she traveled so much, and the only reason that bothered my son was it meant he didn't get to spend as much time with her as he liked.

Alicia, with her usual businesslike manner, was already cutting the thankfully unburnt lasagna and heaping it in generous portions on four plates. I gave her a hug and started to help. I loved dinners here. No, the food wasn't the best, but my cooking was no better, and it sure beat eating alone in front of the TV.

Once we settled down at the dinner table, Martin gave his father a nudge. Immediately an alarm bell went off in my head. I could tell a "go on, ask her" nudge when I saw one.

Frederick cleared his throat, stifled a belch, and said, "Um, Mom, you know how I have that big conference in the city for the next three nights?"

"Yes," I said.

"Well, um, Alicia was going to take care of Martin, but—"

"I'll be really good!" Martin said.

"Wait. What?" I asked, looking from one to the other. Then my eyes settled on Alicia.

The famous scientist shrugged. "I have to go back to CERN. There's some mix-up with the isotopes I can't solve from here. I'm so sorry."

"Three nights!" I turned to Frederick. "But don't you have to go tomorrow?"

My son looked suitably abashed. "I'm sorry. I can take him to school, but then I have to get on the train. This is really important. I'm sorry it's such short notice."

Some words I had said when I first moved here came back to haunt me. *"I can take care of Martin anytime. Just ask. It's no bother. It's not like I have anything else to do."*

Yeah, except catch a murderer who liked slicing people's necks open with hedge clippers.

How the heck was I supposed to do that with Martin around?

"I'll put some lasagna in a Tupperware so you don't have to cook dinner one of the nights," Alicia said.

"And we can go out for burgers the other nights," Martin added helpfully.

"You don't mind, do you?" Frederick asked.

"Don't worry. I won't give you any trouble!" Martin promised.

"I don't mind at all," I lied. Of course I minded, and Martin, out of no malice of his own, would be heaps of trouble. But that wasn't really what bothered me. Neither did the last-minute change of plans it entailed. What I minded was how the heck I was going to carry out a murder investigation while trying to take care of a thirteen-year-old cyclone.

SIX

The strip mall looked deserted. It was well past midnight, and the Cheerville Social Club closed at ten. That was unusually early for a gambling den, but considering so many of its members were senior citizens, I guessed it didn't get much business in the late hours, plus they probably didn't want to attract any undue attention from the police by being the only place open in the strip mall late into the night.

I drove by slowly a couple of times and didn't see any sign of life. No cars were in the parking lot or on the street nearby. Good. That meant the place wasn't being used for any other activities after hours.

Unless these gangsters were good at hiding their vehicles or had dropped off a guard to stay overnight. I had to take care. I parked my car half a block away to be inconspicuous, but it still stood out on the empty street. I grimaced. There was no getting around it. In my younger years, I would have parked a mile away and walked. I couldn't do that anymore and still be in good enough shape to deal with any potential trouble once I got to the target building.

I wished I had enough time to do a proper reconnaissance of this building. It was best to case the building at various times over the course of a night, but if Martin was staying with me tomorrow, I'd have to do all my sneaking around tonight or not at all. Plus, I'd never get to check out the casino's evening crowd like I had intended to.

Of course, I had brought my gun, a 9mm automatic pistol in a locked carrying case as required by state law. Our state was pretty rigid about guns, and you could only pull it out on your own private property or at a firing range. I unlocked the case and tucked the pistol in my pocket. Now I was breaking the law, but sometimes you had to do that for the greater good. My fellow CIA operatives and I had done it so many times, it had almost become the agency motto.

With its comforting weight in the pocket of my sweater, the bulge hidden under my purse, I took a good look around to make sure I was alone and walked to the strip mall. A car passed but didn't slow down. Most civilians don't pay any attention to anything except what directly affects them. As long as a police car didn't pass, I should be all right.

I was in luck and made it to the strip mall without anyone else spotting me. I made a circle around the mall to come at it from the back, passing out of the lit parking lot and storefronts into the relative darkness between the end of the building and a fence cutting it off from a patch of forest. I passed a dumpster, wrinkling my nose at the stench, and came around to the back.

I paused and peeked around the corner. There was a wide strip of pavement, bounded by a chain-link fence, with some parking spaces for employees and delivery vehicles. No cars back here, either, but I bet there were a couple of security cameras. Remaining in the shadows, I pulled a black balaclava out of my purse and put it on. To heighten the disguise, I'd changed into a baggy old sweater I never wore outside the house and a pair of sweat pants and sneakers. I looked ridiculous, I'll admit, but I didn't want to be identified. I planned on becoming a regular visitor to the Cheerville Social Club.

Taking a deep breath and squaring my shoulders, I walked directly to what I estimated to be the back door of the club. As I approached, I saw a security camera fixed above the door, plus a bulb in a bracket that shone a circle of light on the door. If someone was in there, they'd see me for sure, but there was no way to avoid that.

My luck held. No one popped out of the door to put some lead in me. I had even more luck than that. A sticker by the door announced what kind of alarm they had.

That was courteous of them. Announcing there was a burglar alarm was supposed to intimidate me, but it actually made me more confident. I reached into my purse, turned on my phone, brought up a certain classified document, scrolled down to the right entry, then set the phone aside and pulled out my lock pick set and reading glasses.

Yes, I'd reached the point in life where I needed my reading glasses to properly see the lock I was picking.

Opening the door was simplicity itself.

It was dark inside, except for the glowing panel of the security alarm on the wall just beyond the doorway. It was beeping softly, and a little red light flashed on and off. I had thirty seconds to punch in the right code, or the police would be informed. After checking my cell phone, I punched in the number. The beeping stopped, and the flashing red light turned into a steady green one.

Little known fact—all security companies are required to give an override code to the authorities in case the police need to access a property. That information is restricted, of course, but I had gathered lots of interesting restricted material over the years just in case it came in handy someday. Naturally, the authorities are supposed to have a warrant, which I didn't have, but I wasn't about to lose any sleep over that. Laws regarding search warrants were to keep the government from abusing its power, and I support that, but sometimes you had to bend the rules to get the job done. It wasn't like I was breaking into the home of an honest citizen.

Once the alarm was off, I closed the door behind me and switched on the light. I stood in a utilitarian back room with bare concrete walls, a couple of desks, a refrigerator, a large cabinet, and a smaller cabinet with a padlock on it. Not much to look at.

I immediately noticed two things I didn't get to look at, because they weren't there—computers or a Wi-Fi router. If these folks were using computers to track their earnings, they were using laptops they took home with them at the end of the day. Also there was no wireless internet. The best way not to get hacked is to stay offline. I wish some of our government officials would learn that lesson.

First things first—I needed to check the front room to make doubly sure no one was around. A door stood on the opposite wall. I peeked through, gun at the ready, and saw the gaming room, now dark and lonely looking. I've always felt a certain sadness in casinos. Perhaps it's the pervasive desperation of the people there, or perhaps it's just because I know it's a loser's game. But I'd never seen a casino with no people in it before. That made this one look doubly sad. I caught myself wondering if Octavian had started gambling after his wife had died as some sort of coping mechanism.

I pushed him out of my mind and focused on the job. What was I doing thinking of him when I had a murder to solve?

Closing the door to the front room, I got to work. A quick search of the desks turned up nothing but some pens and chewing gum, plus various fliers for takeout restaurants. The large cabinet was filled with snacks to sell to the gamblers, and the refrigerator was stuffed with enough booze to knock out an entire college fraternity. Sitting on top of the cabinet was a large first aid kit. Odd. It looked like something more suited to a ranger's station at a national park rather than a clandestine casino in a sleepy town. Were these folks expecting trouble?

Now I turned my attention to something more interesting—the locked cabinet. Locks have always intrigued me, because locks mean secrets. Even as a little girl, I was obsessed with finding out secrets. I sneaked peeks at my big sister's diary, picking the simple clasp lock with a hairpin, and learned things a little girl shouldn't know about her teenaged big sister. That made me stop looking at her diary, but it sure got me interested in finding out more secrets. I guess that's why I ended up a CIA agent.

I brought out my lock picks again, put on my reading—and lock-picking—glasses, and set to work. A couple of minutes later, I popped open the cabinet.

The laptops weren't there, but something more intriguing was—an old-fashioned ledger. I didn't even know people used ledgers in the First World anymore. But then I realized this gang was so worried about cybersecurity that they hadn't gone digital at all.

I sat down at one of the desks and leafed through it, impressed one of the thugs actually knew how to do accounting the old fashioned way —with a double column and working out the math on paper. I could see the faint traces of the erased work in pencil on the margins. These people were so paranoid they didn't even use the calculators on their phones!

This made me think they were hiding from more than just the police. It takes a lot of work to hack into a phone to the level that you're not just monitoring calls, but seeing what the apps are doing in real time. That made me think of international crime syndicates, the main customers for top-shelf hackers. Could this place be only the local branch of a much larger gambling empire? Having no phones and no computers would mean even if one branch was caught, there wouldn't be anything solid to link it to any other branch. I got the feeling the branches probably didn't even know what other branches existed, the old concept of isolated terrorist cells transferred over to illegal gambling. Clever.

I looked at the electrical outlet next to the desk and got some more support for my theory. The outlet was dusty and obviously hadn't been used for a long time. Moving over to the other desk, I saw the same thing. Nobody was plugging in any laptops at either of these desks.

I went back to studying the ledger. It was mostly sums of the day's earnings, and some pretty hefty earnings they were, too. Near the back, I found something even more interesting. It was a list of addresses with dollar amounts next to each address. Some of these amounts were in the five figures. Next to these amounts were percentages, generally 25 percent or 50 percent, and a column labelled "Due" had a series of dates for each address.

Oh dear. They were playing a double game. Not only did they lure people in to gamble, but they also acted as loan sharks. I wonder if they knew one of their gamblers, Gary Milner, was lending out money too. Perhaps that was why he was so picky about who he lent to, because he didn't want to be discovered.

I skimmed down the addresses, of which there were a good hundred or so, and was intrigued to find 67 Terrace Lane was not among them.

Archibald Heaney did not owe money to the loan sharks.

Did he owe money to Gary?

I took out my phone and took photos of the address list, noting a few addresses showed due dates that had passed. Those would be the ones to really follow up on. Anyone getting leaned on by loan sharks, especially the nasty predators I'd seen running this place, could be pushed to desperate measures.

It was interesting that there were no names on this list. The list was long enough that the accountant couldn't have memorized all the names that went with the addresses, so those names must be linked to a list I wasn't seeing. Another level of security.

Not a very good one, however. Even a simple internet search would bring up many of these names. Not all, though. You could keep your address off the online directories with a request. Who might be doing that, and who was on this list that the loan sharks wanted to keep invisible, intrigued me.

I took a few photos of the accounting then closed the ledger and returned it to the cabinet in the exact same position I had found it. I locked the cabinet and headed out. I'd learned all I could here. On my way out, I cast a nervous glance at the camera. I hadn't seen a recording device inside the building, so it was obviously a remote model, transmitting its picture to a central database for the company. Generally, there wasn't someone watching all the monitors all the time, and that appeared to be the case with this one since the police hadn't shown up to deal with a masked intruder. As long as no one noticed the building had been entered, they would have no reason to review the recording and notice my little visit.

Good thing for me, because I'd probably need to come back with Octavian to see the front room a few more times. My heart did a little flippy-flop at the thought. Purely because of the potential danger, of course.

SEVEN

My grandson, Martin, couldn't figure out why he was being punished. He had come bounding out of school to my car, ready for an afternoon of being spoiled by his grandmother, only to find himself at a meeting of the Cheerville Gardening Society. We hadn't even stopped at his house to get his portable game console, the latest something-or-other that was all the rage and had all his favorite games. He was stuck with me while I puttered about, talking with boring old people—old people so boring that even I found them boring.

The Cheerville Gardening Society met in the garden of a different member each Thursday. The location was listed in the events section of the *Cheerville Gazette*, a section of the newspaper I rarely looked at since it was A, so short, and B, so full of things I didn't want to do.

Like attend a meeting of the Cheerville Gardening Society. Judging from the look of the membership, scattered in little chatting circles on a broad front lawn and a cozy backyard, no one of working age ever did their own gardening in this town. Martin was the youngest person there by a good half century. Even I felt like a spring chicken.

Despite their age, the membership certainly knew its business. The front lawn was carefully manicured, and next to the house was a lush flower bed in a riot of colors. The party spilled over to the backyard, where more flower beds were arranged in a sort of a maze pattern so you could wander on various routes through the yard, admiring the different plants. Most of them I couldn't name, but I didn't need to be a gardening expert to tell our hosts had channeled some serious talent and effort into their work. The conversation between the members was equally esoteric. Every specialty had its own terms and sayings, and it felt like gardeners had their own language.

Of more direct interest to me than figuring out what words like "hydroponics" meant were a pair of topiary bushes flanking the house, both in the shape of poodles. I'd recently learned what topiary meant, and I knew as far as Cheerville was concerned, the term was associated with murder. The poodles were nicely done. I wondered if our hosts or perhaps Archibald had made them.

Someone had handed me a brochure for the Cheerville Gardening Society. Besides some nice pictures, it had a list of officers for the club and noted it met every Thursday. The Topiary Society, which was part of the Gardening Society, met every Wednesday. Archibald had been killed on a Wednesday. Poor fellow didn't get to attend the meeting. There were only two officers listed—Archibald Heaney as president and Tim Harding, my old landlord, as secretary. Interesting.

"These are nicely done," I said to a woman in her seventies who was standing alone near one of the leafy poodles with a plate of éclairs. By the way she was systematically chomping through them, I didn't get the impression she was handing them out. All the éclairs were for her.

"Oh, yes, so sad," she mumbled around a mouthful of gooey sweetness.

"Sad?"

"Archibald made these. He was friends with Mr. and Mrs. Rutgers."

Mr. and Mrs. Rutgers were our hosts. I hadn't

met them yet. There was quite a crowd here, perhaps a hundred people.

"Did he do a lot of people's bushes?"

"Some. I wish I could do it, but my arthritis stops me."

"Didn't Archibald have arthritis too?"

The woman glanced at me. "Him? Oh no, he was as healthy as your grandson here."

So Police Chief Grimal's talk about Archibald being depressed over his arthritis was just fantasy. I had suspected as much.

The woman wandered off, perhaps looking for more éclairs.

We continued to mingle, Martin moping, me looking for people I recognized and not finding anyone. We stopped at the refreshments table, where I managed to get in front of the éclair lady and grab some sweets for Martin.

"Food's good here, eh?" I said encouragingly.

"Can we leave? This is boring."

Oh dear. You know you're in trouble when you can't cheer up a thirteen-year-old boy with free sugar.

"I know this is a bit dull for you, but I want to get into gardening. We're going to make a nice garden for Dandelion."

Martin gave me a suspicious look. "What do you mean we?"

"Oh, I thought you'd like to help since you like Dandelion so much."

"Um, I don't think so. Are we going for hamburgers tonight?"

"Yes, I think you've earned it."

"I've *totally* earned it."

The host and hostess, Mr. and Mrs. Rutgers, came up just then and cheerfully greeted us in the best Cheerville tradition, with plastered-on smiles and an air of casual wealth. I didn't ask if they were related to the founders of the famous university. Judging from the size of their house, I could already figure out the answer.

I didn't get their first names because that was how they introduced themselves—"Mr. and Mrs. Rutgers." Bizarre.

Mrs. Rutgers was leading around a pair of poodles on leashes as she chatted to the guests. The poodles looked like some canine version of topiary. They had a big poof of hair around their heads, shaved forelegs, a ring of hair around their middle, shaved rears, and three poofs of fur on their tails.

"I don't think we've met," she said, all cheery as she shook my hand.

"I'm Barbara Gold. I'm fairly new to

Cheerville. I'm just getting into gardening, and I'd love to come to your meetings regularly. I have so much to learn."

"We're always eager to get new members," Mr. Rutgers said.

"And what's your name?" Mrs. Rutgers asked Martin, leaning down and tousling his hair. I took in a sharp breath. No one tousled Martin's hair— not me, not his parents, not international hit men— no one. To do so was to court death.

"I'm Martin." Martin glowered at her. If looks could kill, she'd have turned into a pile of steaming ash that instant. Her and her little dogs too.

She seemed not to have noticed she had committed a near-fatal error.

"Do you like gardening, Martin?"

"No."

"But flowers are pretty, aren't they?"

"No."

"How about dogs? You like dogs, don't you?"

"Yes."

Ah, the teenage monosyllable. Is there anything more eloquent in its surliness?

"Would you like to go play with my dogs while your grandmother and I chat?"

"No."

"But I thought you liked dogs."

"Those aren't dogs. They're Muppets."

"Such a witty boy!" Mrs. Rutgers hadn't skipped a beat. Mr. Rutgers didn't seem insulted by a thirteen-year-old dismissing his prize poodles, either. Perhaps they hadn't fully processed what Martin had said.

People were good at not noticing things they didn't want to notice. There was an old joke in Washington about President Truman. The story went that he once quipped to a friend that nobody really listened to him at state functions, because no real business ever occurred there, just the usual pleasantries. To prove this, at one Washington reception, he told his friend to follow him as he went around the room greeting people. The two men set out, with Truman shaking everyone's hand and welcoming them to the reception. Each time someone said, "How do you do, Mr. President?" he responded with, "I strangled my wife this morning."

No one made a comment about this startling confession. Some people looked confused, others gave a nervous little laugh, and many more simply smiled and nodded and said something bland in return like, "The economy is looking up, isn't it?"

People expect certain events to run according to a script, and they stick with it. It takes a lot to shake them off of the track they've sent themselves on.

Like a pair of senior citizens rolling around the flower beds, punching each other in the face.

"Cool!" Martin shouted. Suddenly, this whole gardening thing seemed a lot more interesting.

I found it interesting too, not so much for their poor fighting technique—they obviously had never had combat training—but what they were shouting at each other.

"Damn it, Ivan. I told you to back off!"

"It's your fault, Gary. Your fault he's dead!"

The way several people in the crowd glanced at the nearest topiary bush, I knew who Ivan was referring to.

I recognized the two red-faced senior citizens who were destroying Mr. and Mrs. Rutgers' flower bed as being from the secret casino.

They had managed to wreck a good portion of the flower bed, which must be a form of high treason with this crowd, but they hadn't done much damage to each other. They landed punches, sure, but those were poorly aimed, and they weren't even clenching their fists properly or connecting in the right way. It didn't help that their paunches kept them at a fair distance from each other. There's a proper method to punching someone, even if you're fighting from long range. I felt like going over and mansplaining this to them.

A woman of my kill count had earned the right to mansplain, hadn't she?

But I didn't intervene. I was hoping they would shout something that could give me a clue as to what happened to Archibald. It seemed like their energy for shouting had been spent, though, as had most of their energy for fighting. They grunted and smacked at each other a bit more, covered in dirt and fragments of flowers. I started giggling. Call me overly traditional, but there's something innately funny about men with flowers in their hair, especially old men who were pretending they knew how to fight.

Martin was giggling too. I put my arm around his shoulders and he leaned in to me. Such moments of bonding were rare and needed to be treasured.

Sadly, Mr. Rutgers moved in to stop them. He was one of those robust senior citizens who you saw out jogging every morning and who had a fresh, natural tan from some recent beach vacation. He grabbed them both by the collar and pulled them apart. They didn't put up much of a resistance. They looked too exhausted.

"Look what you've done to my daffodils! Now what's all this about?"

Both of them fell silent, glaring at each other with hatred in their eyes.

"Well?" Mr. Rutgers asked.

"Nothing," Ivan muttered.

They creaked to their feet and brushed themselves off. The crowd whispered to themselves and stared. It didn't look like either of them was going to talk.

I found that significant. When people blow up in public, they usually denounce each other, trying to prove to the onlookers they are the one in the right.

But neither of them did that. I wish I had seen who had started the fight. That one obviously couldn't control himself at the sight of the other, even though he wanted to hide the reason why.

Just then, I saw Tim in the crowd, my old landlord and the man who was a fellow topiary expert along with the late, great Archibald Heaney. He was glaring at the two prizefighters with rage shooting out of every pore. I started to move over to him, but he gave me a sharp look and stalked away.

The party began to break up. Nothing breaks up a party of Cheerville's senior citizens like unpleasantness. They had all moved here to bask in pleasantness for the rest of their days and didn't appreciate any nastiness getting in the way of their dreams.

"Oh, why is everyone leaving?" Martin whined. "The party's just getting started!"

"I don't think fistfights are a regular occurrence at the Cheerville Gardening Society."

"That's too bad."

Mr. Rutgers and another man led the combatants to their separate cars and made sure they drove off without any more trouble. I saw Tim heading off too.

"What happened?" I asked a gentleman hobbling by with a cane. I'd briefly chatted with him earlier in the meeting about marigolds.

"Oh, hello again, new girl," he said in a way that was meant to be flirtatious. "Just some nonsense. They're in the local branch of the Topiary Society. It's a subgroup of our thing. Now that Archibald is dead, they both want to be president."

Somehow, I didn't think the fight was over that. Just to pursue that a bit, I said, "Oh, I thought Tim would take over since he's secretary."

"And a fine secretary he is too. Great head for organization. Always consulted with Archibald before and after every meeting. Keeps that group in fine shape. Archibald was more the inspiration and guiding light."

I thought about this. If Tim was in the habit of consulting with Archibald before the Topiary Society's Wednesday meetings, did that mean he was at his house the evening of the murder?

More people started to leave, except for Éclair Lady, who was busy grabbing the last of the desserts before making her departure. Figuring there wasn't much more to find out at this point, I led Martin to my car.

As we drove off to the hamburger joint, Martin still prattling on about the "old people fight," I thought about what I had just witnessed. I'd been looking for overlap between Cheerville's gardeners and gamblers, and I'd found plenty.

I had spent the morning looking up the addresses I had found in the ledger, linking them with names through online directories, and making a quick call to a friend in the CIA to find those who weren't listed. These people had fallen into the trap of borrowing money from the very people who had taken their money in the first place. It amazed me that grown adults could be so foolish.

I focused my attention on those who had large debts that were soon due or past due. The names I got raised some serious red flags. They included

George Whitaker, the sore loser I'd met the day before; Cynthia McAlister, the depressed housewife with the losing streak; and Ivan Dejevsky, who had started a fight with Gary the moneylender while shouting it was Gary's fault Archibald was dead. The list also included Travis Clarke, the county coroner.

Well, that explained why he was so quick to write off Archibald's murder as suicide.

An even more interesting fact was the amount Clarke owed was past due but had been crossed out with a single line. I presumed that meant he no longer owed the money. So why had his debt been forgiven? It was for fourteen thousand dollars, a large amount for a state employee to suddenly cough up, and I seriously doubt he won that gambling. Was this his reward for declaring Archibald's death a suicide?

One name was missing from the list entirely—Grimal's. Whatever the reason he was covering up Archibald's murder, it was not because the police chief owed money to organized crime. Tim and Gary were also not on the list.

I was relieved to see Octavian's name wasn't on the list, either. That probably accounted for his sunny disposition. It's hard to keep your chin up when you're being leaned on by loan sharks.

Archibald had been caught up with illegal gambling and associated with people who owed money to loan sharks. Somehow that had led to his death. But he hadn't owed money, so why did someone go after him? Had maxing out those credit cards been enough to cover his debts, or had he borrowed from Gary?

It was hard to figure this out, though, because Martin kept retelling the fight he'd seen in an excited voice that commanded attention.

"Did you see who threw the first punch?" I asked.

"Yeah, the guy called Ivan."

I nodded. That was what I thought.

While we were chowing down on hamburgers, my cell phone rang. Octavian.

"Hi, Barbara. What are you up to?"

"I'm with my grandson at Taco Burger."

That's right, it was called Taco Burger. You got your burger in a taco shell with hot sauce. Delicious if you remember to take your heartburn medication. Yes, I know I said I had an iron stomach earlier, but even I have limits.

"Oh right, it's dinner time. I better get myself something to eat. I forget sometimes. I haven't even gone to the supermarket. There's nothing in the house."

Octavian might have been my first date since Carter was president, but I still knew when a man was inviting himself over.

I gave him the address. He knew Archibald, and stuck as I was with Martin for the next three days, I needed to combine work and play if I was going to crack this case.

Octavian being the work part. Really.

EIGHT

Octavian showed up within fifteen minutes. Cheerville was a small town, after all, so there was a good chance he didn't break the speed limit to make it over to see me. He came striding up to our table wearing that winning smile of his that showed his excellent-but-actually-real teeth. Before even saying hello to me, he turned to Martin and said, "This must be the world's greatest grandson I've heard so much about. You need to clean behind your ears, though."

He performed the old "pull the coin from behind the ear" trick.

Martin gave him a patient smile. It wasn't nearly a good enough trick to impress his jaded generation.

But Octavian wasn't finished. He showed him the quarter resting in his palm then closed it and reopened it. Now it was a dime. He closed his hand again, and when he reopened it, he was holding a nickel. Then he turned it into a penny. Martin grinned.

"This is what happens with savings, my friend. They dwindle away. That's why you have to live for today. But sometimes…"

At this he closed his hand again, and when he reopened it, there was an old Indian Head penny sitting there.

"Sometimes old money can be valuable. These coins are pretty rare these days. Here, take it."

Martin's grin grew wider and he reached for it. Octavian pulled back. "Hey, you should know better than to take money from strangers! Oh wait, I'm not a stranger, because your grandma has told me all about you. She has told you all about me, right?"

"No."

"Oh." Octavian looked discomfited. He rallied quickly. "Well, we only just met. She's quite good at Seniors Yoga."

"Seniors Yoga?" Martin gave me a "you're such a nerd" look.

"That's right," he said, plunking the Indian

Head penny in front of Martin and flicking it so it spun on its side. The waitress came over, and he ordered a Taco Burger. I feared for his digestive system.

"So what have you folks been up to this afternoon?" he asked once the waitress went off.

Martin brightened. "We saw a fight!"

Octavian cocked his head. "Really?" Fights were rare in Cheerville.

"Yes, between Gary and Ivan," I told him. "Apparently, they were fighting over who gets to run the local chapter of the Topiary Society now that Archibald has… passed on."

He shook his head and waved his hand to negate that idea, just as I suspected. "Those two don't care about that."

"Really?" I asked, acting innocent.

"Yeah, it's…" His gaze slid to Martin. "Complicated."

His order came, and we ate, talking about nothing in particular. Octavian seemed eager to make a good impression with Martin, probably to get in better with me, and he more or less succeeded. Martin has little time for old people, and even less for things like Seniors Yoga, but Octavian was good with the jokes and a few more magic tricks. I wondered if he'd be able to pull the murderer out of a hat. That would make my life easier.

Later, when Martin headed off to the bathroom, I took the opportunity to ask Octavian about the fight.

"So why were those two rolling around in the garden, smacking at each other?"

Octavian chuckled. "I would have liked to have seen that."

"Martin certainly enjoyed it. But why did they do it?"

"They're always sniping at one another. By the way, would you like to go to the club this evening?"

"I can't. I have Martin," I said, feeling a little tug I told myself was disappointment at not being able to pursue the case. "We can go tomorrow during school hours, though."

"All right," he said. "Hopefully those two idiots won't be there."

Hopefully they will be, I thought to myself.

"I just can't believe two men their age would get into a juvenile brawl," I said to get Octavian back on track.

"Gary and Ivan fell out over money."

"Oh, really?"

Octavian made a face. "Ivan doesn't know how to play. He doesn't understand the horses, and he keeps plunking down money on duds. He doesn't have a system. Gary and Ivan used to be friends, and Gary lent him some cash to cover his debts. Ivan paid it back, but when he started losing again, Gary offered to lend him more money. Ivan took it the wrong way, like Gary was being condescending. I don't know, maybe he was, but Ivan got hypersensitive about losing when Gary is one of the luckiest in our club. So anyway, I guess they didn't patch things up this afternoon."

"Did you ever loan money to Ivan?"

"Oh, heck no. 'Neither a borrower nor a lender be' as old Will Shakespeare used to say. That's how friendships are ruined."

I studied Octavian. He looked like he was telling the truth, and since he didn't owe money to the loan sharks, I doubted he was involved in the mess that entangled some of the others. I decided to take a chance. The longer it took to catch the killer, the greater the chances they'd be able to slip away.

"Ivan said something strange. He said it was Gary's fault someone was dead. I got the impression he meant Archibald."

As soon as I said it, Octavian's face transformed completely. He went from his usual smiling self to a mask of travesty. He bowed his head and gave a little nod.

"Maybe. Maybe," he mumbled.

"But whatever could that mean?" I asked, glancing in the direction of the bathroom, hoping Martin would take some time in there.

Octavian sighed and rubbed his eyes. "Gary has done very well for himself in his hardware business. He has stores in half a dozen towns. Plus, he has the Midas touch when it comes to the casino. He really knows how to work the horses and dogs, really knows how to play the odds. And he's generous. I know he lent Archibald money a couple of times. Maybe Archibald was like Ivan; he borrowed from Gary, but that humiliated him. It hurt his pride so badly that when he kept losing, he couldn't stand to take another loan, and took his own life instead."

I nodded sadly, pretending to believe this story. I certainly believed Octavian felt it was true. But Archibald hadn't killed himself; he had been murdered. By Gary, angered over lack of payment? Had Archibald taken all those cash advances from his credit cards to try and keep up? Running a hardware store, Gary certainly would know how to use hedge clippers, but then again, so did most of my suspects. And of course, killing someone who owes you money is a poor way to collect.

Maybe Archibald thought of another way out.

Maybe he threatened to go to the police and expose the whole thing. Maybe he'd even finger Gary as some sort of accomplice and get him arrested. That would get rid of his debt to Gary and get rid of the temptation to continue gambling in one stroke. Gary could have come to his house, demanding payment, and Archibald could have made his threat. Gary panicked, a struggle ensued, and Archibald ended up dead.

Hmmm, pretty thin.

I saw Octavian wiping his eyes.

"You all right?" I asked.

He shook his head. "No, not really. Archibald was my friend, and at our age, we lose too many friends. I used to be able to handle it, but after Louise passed, it's been hitting me harder and harder. It feels like my life is closing in on me. My circle of friends gets smaller every year."

"What about other family?"

Octavian gave a sad smile. "I have two sons and a daughter. Wonderful. They turned out wonderful. And I've been a granddad four times over already. But they're scattered all over the country."

"When James died, I moved here. I never thought I'd end up in a place like this, but now I treasure every moment with my son and daughter-in-law, and especially my grandson. Maybe you should move to be with them. Grandchildren are such a blessing."

A loud belch told us my little blessing had returned.

Martin plopped down in his seat. "We're going for ice cream after this, right?"

Octavian laughed. "Sure thing, kiddo."

As Martin got into my car, I paused with Octavian outside to arrange which ice cream parlor we'd meet at. He took the time to ask me a question.

"Look, I know you didn't know him," he said, looking uncomfortable, "but if you'd like to come to Archibald's memorial service, I know you'd be welcome. It's tomorrow at noon. I mean, you'd get to know some of the gang better, and it... well, never mind. It's silly to ask. Why would you want to?"

"Of course I'll go."

I'd have gone even if I didn't have a case to solve. This kind man was trying to ask for emotional support at a time when he clearly needed it. Men weren't very good at asking for that; they've been trained not to. That halfhearted offer and immediate retraction had been the best Octavian could do.

I gave him a peck on the cheek. That certainly

seemed to cheer him up. "Text me the information, and I'll meet you for coffee beforehand."

When I turned back to my car, I saw Martin looking at us through the window in astonishment. He giggled all through ice cream.

———

THAT EVENING, while Martin did his homework, I took the opportunity to study the photos I had taken of the murder scene. The recently washed wall intrigued me, but there was nothing to see. The killer had cleaned it thoroughly, so I turned my attention to the footprints in the soft soil.

After putting on my reading glasses and expanding the photos, I could see there were two styles of shoes—a pair of treaded sneakers and a pair of flat-soled shoes, probably dress shoes. The sneakers were obviously Archibald's. No one is going to putter around the garden and use power tools in flat-soled shoes. I could also tell another way. One of the flat-soled footprints was in the dirt close to the wall and twice as deep as the others. The killer had obviously hosed down the wall after taking care of Archibald and unwittingly stepped in the mud he or she had created. That mud had dried, preserving the footprint. Unfortunately, only part of the heel had hit that muddy spot, so it would be difficult to determine shoe size from it.

I wasn't an expert on these subtleties of police research. There were people who were, people Police Chief Grimal would have on speed dial, but I couldn't rely on him. I was on my own with this one.

I puzzled over the footprints for a while longer, trying to tease information from faint traces in the soil. Two of the more visible, and slightly deeper, of the sneaker prints faced the topiary bush. Were those made while Archibald stood trimming? Several bits of branch lay around, seeming to confirm my thesis.

In one of my photos, I had put my own foot next to two fairly good specimens of each footprint for scale. I wore a size eight, and both were considerably bigger than mine. They looked about James's size, and he had worn a ten and a half. So most likely, the killer was a man. Few women had that shoe size, although I couldn't discount the possibility.

The other footprints were less clear, a chaotic pattern of sneakers and flat-soled shoes overlapping one another and facing all directions. That was probably Archibald moving around a bit before the attack, and then the struggle between him and his killer.

I tracked through the footprints one by one on maximum zoom. Luckily, I had my camera already set to the highest resolution. I'm old fashioned in some ways, and so I always kept my camera at that setting so I could print photos. Most people didn't do that anymore, and that was a shame. They ended up missing important details in crime scenes.

Such as the exact spot Archibald and his attacker were standing when Archibald had his neck gashed by his own hedge clippers.

It took a while for me to see, but when I did, the pair of prints almost popped out of the screen at me. They stood at the center of a blur of prints, made as the two fought over the hedge clippers, struggling in a deadly embrace before the attacker broke free and was able to swing them at Archibald. The flat-soled attacker had put some effort into it, his or her back right foot pressed down at the toe, and the front left foot made a print deeper than the others as he or she put more weight on it. Archibald's sneakers had left a deep impression on the heels as he leaned back to avoid being struck, and then continued the motion as he fell back, his neck spurting blood.

It must have been quite a mess. Even a couple

of days after the crime, I'd seen what looked like traces of blood on the ground and leaves of Archibald's half-trimmed shamrock bush. The killer must have been covered in it. He or she—probably he—was lucky not to have been spotted leaving the crime scene looking like that. I assumed the killer hadn't brought along a change of clothes, stuffing the bloody ones in a bag. People planning murders did that sometimes, but this had the hallmarks of sudden impulse. The killer had had the presence of mind to clean the wall, however.

Why? Why stay put at a crime scene for an extra couple of minutes to clean a wall? Perhaps the killer had accidentally touched the wall and left bloody fingerprints?

Then something else struck me. The pattern of the killer's footprints—right foot back, left foot forward—was the natural attack stance for a left-handed person. Plus, the wall was to the killer's right, meaning he or she swung from the left to the right, spraying blood to the right and onto the wall.

I checked the distance from the killer's stance to the wall then looked up the length of your average hedge clippers. A hedge clipper's blades ranged from thirteen to thirty inches. I also learned topiary experts only use hedge clippers, when they use them at all, for the rough work right at the beginning of spring, after which they use pruning shears. Investigating crimes led me to know all sorts of odd bits of information that would, hopefully, never be useful again. I don't think I could take another hedge-clipper murder.

Anyway, there was enough room for a right-handed swing, so it wasn't a right-handed person having to swing left-handed. It was a left-handed attacker.

I kicked myself for not seeing this before. If I had, I would have checked out every man, woman, and criminal thug in that covert casino to see which hand they favored.

So I had a left-handed attacker with a shoe size of around ten or eleven, someone who had killed on impulse but had the presence of mind to clean the wall but not wipe away the footprints. A reasonably cool-headed amateur.

I wondered why I didn't see any other footprints in the area. Whoever had found him—I didn't even know who that was since I was really working in the dark on this one—had not come close to the body. From the description of the wound, Archibald had been so obviously dead that the person had fled to call the authorities rather than bend down and check on the body. When the police and EMTs arrived, they had obviously not wanted to contaminate the scene. That was standard procedure. So the cover-up came later.

But if the coroner and police chief decided to cover this whole thing up, why hadn't they wiped the footprints? Perhaps they didn't think anyone would investigate?

My next task was to do some more internet research. My first stop was digging up what I could find on Travis Clarke, the county coroner who had signed off on the obviously erroneous conclusion that Archibald had killed himself. Clarke owed money to the loan sharks and had been past due until his account was wiped clean.

State employee salaries are public since they are paid by the taxpayers, and I discovered Clarke earned sixty thousand a year. There was no way he had paid off a fourteen-thousand-dollar loan himself in one lump sum. The notation hadn't shown him paying it off bit by bit. It simply showed a line through the amount as if it had been paid in full. I suspected the loan sharks had most likely forgiven his debt in exchange for covering up the murder.

Could he be the murderer? Unlikely. Even if he was in charge of the investigation, he would have made the "suicide" look more believable. As a coroner, he was an expert on death and evidence of wrongful death. He would not have made such a basic mistake as killing someone with hedge clippers. Martin would call that a "n00b move."

Then I discovered something even juicier—a wedding announcement from fifteen years ago. Clarke had married Alice Grimal. A quick check revealed she was Police Chief Grimal's sister.

Clarke and Grimal were related, and they had conspired to cover up a murder.

But I still did not think they were the killers. Like Clarke, Grimal wouldn't have killed someone in such a sloppy fashion, and I couldn't picture him as a murderer, anyway. He was too weak.

So why were they covering up the murder? For a measly fourteen thousand dollars? That didn't make sense. If Clarke was that desperate, he could spill everything to his brother-in-law, and Grimal could shut the place down. The loan sharks wouldn't be so stupid as to take vengeance out on the relative of the local police chief.

No, there was a more likely explanation—that Grimal knew all about the gambling operation and was taking bribes. When the murder happened, he probably got some shut-up money, as did his brother-in-law.

I needed to tread carefully. If the law was against me, I wasn't sure who to turn to even if I did find the murderer. I also didn't know how far up this went. I'd already determined this was a professional operation that almost certainly had branches in other towns and cities, perhaps dozens or even hundreds. The corruption might reach up to the state level or beyond.

I might've not been simply fighting a group of casino operators and loan sharks; I might've been fighting some very powerful political figures.

If I interfered with their operation, the next set of hedge clippers might be aimed at me.

NINE

The memorial service couldn't have been lovelier. Archibald certainly had a lot of friends, and since so many of them were gardening and topiary buffs, he had one of the lushest memorial services I had ever attended. The best smelling too.

It was held on the spacious back lawn of the funeral home of Charles Fowler, a friend of mine from my reading group. Oddly enough, poor old Charles had been a suspect in the last murder I solved, when Lucien Rogers had dropped dead from poisoning at a meeting of that very same group. I was happy to say Charles had done an excellent job cleaning up his corpse and that he'd had nothing to do with turning him into a corpse in the first place.

Charles had done a good job here too. Thankfully there was no open casket (I hate those), just a lectern decorated with a large photo of Archibald, rows of seats, and a buffet off to one side.

The gardeners and topiary experts had done the rest. Flanking the lectern was a series of splendid wreaths donated by various members of the two societies of which Archibald had been such a large part, plus a floral arch over the front of the central aisle between the rows of chairs. Arranged around the area were several smaller examples of topiary in pots. Angels figured prominently, plus a scattering of cheerful animals and a few geometric shapes. I saw no shamrocks like the one Archibald had been tending when he had been killed. His luck had run out.

Unfortunately, Octavian led me to the front row, where I wouldn't be able to observe anyone. I recognized Archibald's two grown children who I'd spotted at his house, plus another man, a little younger, I suspected was his third child. We sat down near them. They talked in low tones, and I couldn't hear much of what they said over the buzz of the crowd. I could tell they were still talking about their late father's credit cards and bank account, though.

Poor kids. No matter how old you were, it still

couldn't feel good to find out something embarrassing about your father. Especially when you think he killed himself over it.

I felt a twinge of guilt. How would they feel when I proved to them their father had been murdered? Ten times worse, and yet I couldn't let his murderer go unpunished.

Before the service began, I took the opportunity to scan the crowd for people I recognized. Once the service started, I'd be stuck facing forward and wouldn't be able to see anyone's reactions. I managed to spot most of the gamblers and gardeners I'd met. Ivan and Gary were there, both sporting black eyes and standing on opposite sides of the yard. I felt a chill when I noticed Tim Harding, the quiet landlord, move up and speak to Ivan.

After dropping my grandson off at school that morning, I'd gone to the county records office to look up the owner of the property where the Cheerville Social Club was located. It was owned by Samantha Ingold. A quick internet search turned up only one Samantha Ingold in the state, and she was a freshman at the city university. A property owner barely out of high school? Unlikely.

I did some more digging, both online and at the county records office, and found a certain Tim Harding had sold it to her a few months before for a dollar. I also found Tim had once been married to a woman whose maiden name was Ingold. They had divorced a few years before.

So Tim had given the property to his daughter as a gift, a gift of the selfish variety. He'd given it to her to mask the fact that he was, in all likelihood, the real owner. It would certainly be him collecting the rent and dealing with the tenants. And I bet those tenants were paying a lot more than the usual rate. I wonder if they let him win at roulette too.

So Tim had a financial stake in the business. He'd want to keep it protected. I remembered that glare he gave me when I tried to speak with him after the fight. Could he have been the murderer? How could I prove it?

Tim and Ivan sat down together. Gary shot a nasty look in their direction but did not go over. I also spotted Cynthia McAlister in the crowd, sitting alone and looking sad, as well as George Whitaker, also sitting alone and busy texting on his phone. Some people will text anywhere, and given his poor manners, it didn't surprise me one bit.

I also saw the final member of my hit list— Travis Clarke, the county coroner. I'd never met him before, only studied his photo in a newspaper article I'd dug up, but I was sure it was him, sitting near the back and wearing a pair of sunglasses while shifting nervously in his seat. I noticed he kept glancing to the right and left. While his eyes remained hidden, I suspected he was watching Ivan and Gary. That little explosion of rage at the gardening meeting had sent ripples through Cheerville society, and the last thing someone involved with a murder needed was people sending ripples.

My observations kept getting interrupted by Octavian making small talk. I couldn't act too suspiciously and had to spend half my time looking at him instead of a crowd containing a murderer. It was most frustrating. So far in our short acquaintance, it was the first time I'd wanted him to shut up and go away. Not his fault, the poor fellow, but I really didn't have time for him at the moment.

And my time to observe the crowd had run out. People began to take their seats. Conversation ebbed away as people looked toward the lectern with an air of expectation. I turned to face forward.

Ricardo Morales hovered near the lectern, looking nervous and shuffling a few notecards in his hands. A Baptist minister stood nearby.

The minister spoke first, giving a standard sermon about life and death and faith. He also added a few personal details about how Archibald had been a regular member of the Cheerville

Baptist Church. I suspected the good preacher didn't know about Archibald's gambling habit. I wasn't a Baptist, but I'd heard they took a pretty dim view of games of chance. Ah well, as an African Methodist minister in a particularly rough area of Los Angeles once told me, "If the people in my congregation were without sin, there would be no need for them to come to church."

Besides, a bit of gambling on the side was nothing compared to the sin of murder. Some nice, respectable member of the prosperous community of Cheerville had committed the gravest sin of all.

The minister kept it short, and then Ricardo Morales took over. He gave a nervous speech about how Archibald had been a good friend and upstanding member of the community who had beautified the city. He gave a few anecdotes about their time together as friends and about the volunteer work he did beautifying the lawns of the local seniors home and library. It was all pretty standard. I'd never liked memorial services, particularly the speeches. Everyone already knew what the deceased had accomplished, and any jokes inevitably fell flat. Still, it was tradition, and you couldn't say goodbye without some sort of send-off.

I listened with half an ear, hoping to catch an important detail while paying more attention to

Ricardo's mannerisms. Why was he so nervous? Simple stage fright or something else? Most likely the latter. He kept glancing at Ivan, probably worried he'd cause more trouble. Ricardo hadn't been at the gardening meeting, but the way gossip ran through Cheerville like wildfire, he would have almost certainly heard about the fight.

Ricardo was also talking faster than normal, as if he was in a hurry to get through the speech. I guessed he wanted to finish this service without any trouble.

But whatever was going through that handsome Hispanic head was not fear of being caught for murder. When he gestured, it was with his right hand. When he shuffled his notes, it was the right hand that was dominant. Ricardo Morales was right-handed and therefore not the murderer. How much he knew about Archibald's death was another question. I seemed to have uncovered quite a nasty little web in that suburban strip mall.

Only when Ricardo's speech came to a conclusion did he give me something of interest.

"And as hard as he worked in his garden and in the gardens of so many others, Archibald Heaney always knew how to relax with a nice glass of wine. The rich, fruity flavors of Spanish Rioja were his favorite. There are several bottles of his favorite vintage over at the buffet. I think he'd be very happy if we all got a glass and drank a toast in his honor."

A toast. Perfect. All the righties toasting with their right hand and all the lefties toasting with their left hand. Thank you, Ricardo.

Everyone moved over to the buffet. It took a fair amount of self-control on my part not to rush over there, grab a glass, and stand on the table so I could see everyone. That probably wouldn't do my reputation much good.

We gathered around. There must have been more than a hundred people there, and it was going to be impossible to see everyone. Three young waiters had already poured wine into glasses, and everyone went en masse to pick them up. Already, people were walking away with glasses, while others stood in the way of my line of sight. We were in the middle of a shuffling crowd moving toward the table. I'd never been so dissatisfied with my short stature. Why couldn't I have been six foot ten, at least for today? This golden opportunity was turning into a disaster.

I'd already taken Ricardo off my list, although he hadn't ever been a strong suspect in the first place. That left Tim, Ivan, Gary, Travis, Cynthia, and George.

Cynthia walked past us, carrying a wine glass in her right hand. Good girl. Your life may be a mess, but you didn't slash someone's throat open with hedge clippers. Points to you.

I saw George move away from the table, his body obscured by the crowd. I almost wept with frustration. Then I saw Tim come right past us. My heart leapt. Here was my star suspect, the man who had rented property to the casino, the man who habitually met with the victim on the day of the week he had been killed, about to pass so close I could reach out and touch him.

Then my heart sank. He was carrying a wine glass in each hand. I never took him for a lush.

Oh wait, not a lush. He was heading back to Ivan, who had remained in his seat. I glanced around for Gary and saw him nearby with a wine glass in his right hand. Ivan may have thought it was Gary's fault for Archibald dying, but if he was, it was only indirectly.

That left Tim, Ivan, Travis, and George.

Octavian and I got our glasses, and I lingered by the table, hoping to catch sight of another suspect. Motioning with his wine glass—held, I am glad to say, in his right hand—Octavian made a move to lead me away then stopped when I didn't follow. Instead, I engaged in small talk with him, ignoring his body language telling me to move out of the way and stop blocking traffic.

"Let's go back to our seats," he finally said.

I let out a sigh of frustration. I couldn't think of an excuse not to, and so I slowly followed him.

Slowly enough to catch sight of Travis Clarke, county coroner, pick up a wine glass with his right hand. Tick another one off.

Ricardo stood at the lectern, a wine glass in his right hand. The Baptist minister stood nearby. Unlike everyone else, he didn't have a glass. Perhaps he was a teetotaler. Perhaps he objected to Archibald's supposed suicide. It didn't matter. Thankfully, he wasn't a suspect.

"To Archibald Heaney!" Ricardo declared, raising his glass.

"To Archibald Heaney!" the crowd responded.

I made a slow turn, as if toasting the entire crowd. I caught sight of George Whitaker, the angry loser from the casino, raising his glass in his left hand.

Bingo.

Bingo?

I still couldn't see Tim and Ivan. George made a good suspect—short tempered, owed a lot of money, knew Archibald well. Was he my man?

Impossible to tell without checking on Tim and Ivan.

Just then, I had a stroke of luck. Someone I didn't recognize came up and talked to Octavian. I slipped away while his back was turned.

I made my way through the crowd to the far edge of the seating, and there I saw Tim and Ivan standing a little apart from the rest of the gathering. Ivan was holding his wine glass in his right hand and had just finished knocking back the last of it.

Tim was holding it in his left.

Oh great, two lefties in my list of suspects? What were the chances?

I had a way to figure out who did it, but it would depend on Ivan being impulsive again.

I was also banking on the hope that the murderer wouldn't try something silly in front of all those people.

Oh, and I had my gun in my purse. Naturally.

I walked right up to Ivan with a cross look on my face.

"Well done," I told him.

Ivan looked confused. Tim looked wary.

"Well done smacking that man. He has no esprit de corps."

Understanding dawned on both their faces.

"You're darn right about that," Ivan said. "People have to help each other out."

"You know, I asked Gary for a little loan yesterday, just fifty dollars so I didn't have to go to the ATM. I didn't want to miss any races. I could have paid him back that very same day, and he turned up his nose and walked away like I was the scum of the earth! That's why Octavian and I left early."

"Typical," Ivan grumbled. Tim nodded eagerly.

Oh yes, Tim, I thought. *You want me to believe this story, don't you?*

I took the next step.

"And not lending money to poor Archibald. They told me what Gary said to him. What was it? It was so rude I can't even remember."

"'This is the very last time, you loser,'" Ivan quoted helpfully.

It's funny, but I always feared getting old. I feared people would start underestimating me. And they do. A sweet little old lady like me, with her practical shoes and her mild manners. People drop their guard, even other senior citizens. Growing old may very well be the best thing that can happen in a CIA agent's career.

"And it's not like Archibald and I were the only ones he was rude to. I'm so glad you thumped him," I said, putting a hand on his chest. I may have been a few years older than Ivan, but at his age, any man wants female attention, especially after trying to prove their prowess in a fight.

Ivan blushed. "Thank you."

"I'm surprised George didn't do it first. He must have been livid."

"He almost did right then and there."

"What a fink," Tim said, raising his left hand to take a sip of his glass. "And now we've lost the best topiary expert in the state."

And then it all fell into place.

George had mentioned he couldn't get a loan. What he meant was he couldn't get a loan from Gary to make his payment to the loan sharks. Getting into debt with an individual to pay off a casino wasn't the smartest move unless the casino was run by obvious predators. The "then and there" Ivan referred to was that Archibald and George had asked for loans at the same time. He'd given money to Archibald but not George. George had said as much when he complained about how "some people get preferential treatment with that guy."

So George had gone over to Archibald's house to see if he could borrow some of that borrowed money for himself. When Archibald said no, George got desperate. At first he probably only

wanted to threaten Archibald with the hedge clippers, but Archibald kept refusing out of desperation
over his own financial straits, and then George's
temper got the better of him. The hedge clippers
swung down and killed the best topiary expert in
the state…

On the night of the meeting of the Topiary
Society. George wasn't in the Topiary Society—"I
have better things to do than fiddle around with
plants," he'd said—and didn't know this. He also
didn't know Tim, being secretary of that society,
went over to see Archibald just before the meeting
to make plans for that evening's schedule.

George had already killed him. Tim found the
body and didn't report it because he panicked.
What if the police suspected murder and the casino
was discovered?

But surely he knew the county coroner was a
member of the casino. An important businessman
such as Tim would know all the major officials. He
was involved in local politics. So he tidied up the
crime scene a little. Not well enough, being an
amateur in everything but topiary and real estate.

But why clean up the blood on the wall at all?
Even cleaning it off left a clue that it had been there
in the first place, because anyone would reasonably
assume that with the gore all around the body, at

least some would get on the wall. Tim didn't clean up the blood because it was blood. He cleaned it up because of something else.

I saw George standing alone, sipping his wine not far away. I waved him over.

A glance at Tim's reaction told me I was right. He went ghastly pale. Poor fellow. Perhaps he needed some more of this lovely wine. I glanced at Tim's feet. He had big feet to hold up that tall, lanky body. A size thirteen at least. George's feet, on the other hand, were about normal for a six-foot-tall man—size ten or eleven, I'd say.

George walked up. "Hello, Barbara. Planning on going to the club later?"

"Yes. Did you know that even if you cut some-one's throat, it takes a couple of minutes for them to die?"

George blanched. "What?"

"They choke on their own blood, desperately trying to get air into their lungs. They stay conscious for at least a minute, longer than you stuck around. You wiped your prints off the hedge clippers and took off in a panic. He was dying, of that you were sure, but what you didn't realize was that he had enough life left in him to write your name in his own blood on the wall."

George sputtered. Tim looked about to faint.

Ivan stared at me like I was some crazy lady pushing a shopping cart down the middle of the highway, muttering to herself.

"Don't worry," I continued. "Tim showed up just afterward to plan a meeting of the Topiary Society. They have one every Wednesday night, you see. He saw the name and hosed it off so he could protect his little business. Just how much do you charge those bookies in rent, Tim?"

Tim sat down hard on one of the chairs, some of the red wine sloshing out of the glass and onto his hand. George took a step forward.

"You better watch what you say to people, you b—"

Ivan stepped between us, his chest puffed out in an attempt to make it bigger than his belly. So sweet.

"Watch how you speak to the lady, George, or I'll teach you some manners. Now what's going on here?"

"Nothing. She's crazy!" George's voice didn't sound so tough now. It sounded on the verge of hysteria. Tim leapt up and started walking away, his long legs eating up the ground. He pulled his cell phone from his pocket.

I walked away too. I had enough circumstantial evidence to call the state police and get them both pulled in for questioning. Tim would at least be charged as an accessory for the casino. It would be hard for him to feign ignorance of what went on at his own property. With the photos I had from the ledger, I could get George investigated for murder and Tim as an accessory to that crime too. And I'd seen enough tough guys break under questioning that I knew those two idiots wouldn't last an hour.

But their arrest could wait. If they ran, they wouldn't get far, and any alibis they tried to make up at this point would fall flat.

I needed to stop those casino people from getting away. I had a feeling that was who Tim had called.

Poor Octavian, getting stood up like that. I decided to make some excuse that I felt emotionally overwhelmed and had to leave. He'd probably still feel somewhat jilted, but it was his fault for asking a girl out on a date to a memorial service.

TEN

The parking lot of the strip mall was about half full when I arrived. I noticed a couple of cars leaving as I drove into the lot. A quick glance showed none of the criminals were inside the vehicles. As I parked, half a dozen people came out of the Cheerville Social Club, heading for their cars and looking disappointed. I spotted someone I vaguely recognized.

"What's the matter? Lose big?"

The man gave me a suspicious look then recognized me and shrugged.

"No, they're closing for the day. Something about an exterminator coming."

Oh dear. I didn't like the wording of that excuse. I put on my reading glasses so I could see the sights on my pistol and unzipped my purse so I could draw it quickly.

Just as I got to the door, another group of gamblers came out.

"Want to come to my house and play some poker?" one asked the others.

I slipped through the crowd and through the front door before Lance, the bouncer, could shut it.

"We're closed today, ma'am," Lance said. Then a spark of recognition lit up his eyes. Tim had warned him about me. He reached for the inside pocket of his sports coat.

I was quicker. I drew my pistol from my purse, flicked off the safety, and leveled it at him.

"Easy there. Let's have a little chat, shall we?" I said in my nicest little-old-lady voice while treating him to a smile. That, combined with the gun, always knocks them off-kilter.

The man stood a foot above me and must have weighed more than twice as much, all of it muscle, but my gun made a great equalizer. What was the saying in the Old West? "God made man, but Sam Colt made them equal." Something like that.

The man stiffened and raised his hands above his head. I had already stepped a bit inside to keep out of sight of the people in the parking lot. Since I didn't hear any gasps or shouts, I figured I was still not making a scene. Good. I liked my anonymity in this town.

I dropped my purse and reached into the guard's coat to retrieve his weapon, a slim little 9mm automatic. I turned off the safety and, covering him with both guns, ordered him to open the inner door and enter the casino. I came in right behind him, the outer door slamming shut behind us.

And that was when everything went wrong.

I saw the guy hidden behind the door in time not to get my head shot off. Just as he was raising his pistol, I brought up my left arm and smacked him in the wrist with my captured pistol. If I was younger, the blow would have been harder, and the man's gun would have flown out of his grip. Instead, his arm jerked up and the bullet that was about to go in my brain planted itself in the ceiling. On instinct, I fired with my other pistol just as Lance, the bouncer, ducked away. He cried out, clutching his side and falling to the floor.

I spun, meaning to pump a bullet in the gut of the man who had tried to shoot me, but I was too slow. I was only able to turn half the way before he grabbed my wrist with his free hand and, with his gun hand, hit my other arm. Pain lanced up my arm, and that gun clattered to the floor.

I still held my own gun in my right hand. I hissed with pain as he tightened his grip. In another second, I'd drop it for sure.

So I twisted my wrist and tried to shoot him in the ribs.

He was too good for that trick. He yanked on my arm, and I only managed to hit the wall, fragments of concrete stinging us both.

He leveled his own gun at me.

There was nothing quite like the sight of a gun barrel pointed straight at you. The barrel of a 9mm wasn't really that big, but when you were staring into its darkness, it seemed like it took up the entire world. It was like a vortex that threatened to suck you in. It was hypnotic. Most people froze when they saw it.

I didn't.

"Law enforcement," I said, managing to keep my voice remarkably calm, if I do say so myself.

"You? Police? Come on," he said. A third thug came running up and bent over Lance.

"She got him through the side. I'll grab the first aid kit. Get rid of her."

The man ran off to the back room. I looked back at the one holding the gun on me. The bouncer at our feet groaned and writhed.

"You kill a member of law enforcement, and they will track you down," I stated.

The man's eyes narrowed. His gun did not waver.

"You're too old. You move like you got training, though."

"So do you. Ex-army?"

"I'm asking the questions. Are you ex-police?" Doubt laced his voice. I didn't look the part. I've never looked the part. I've endured decades of superior officers doing a double take as they looked at my CV. Yes, CIA agents have CVs. You've never seen one, and you never will.

"I'm ex-CIA."

The man snorted, but he still looked at me with a mixture of doubt and wariness.

For half a minute, there was silence. I glanced around the room. It looked as sad and lonely as it had the night I'd snuck in. All the TVs were off, and the roulette wheel had been taken off its base and encased in bubble wrap. The door to the back room stood open, and I saw a dolly sitting in the office. As I had suspected, Tim's warning call had prompted them to skip town.

The third thug came back with the first aid kit.

"You haven't smoked her yet?"

"Says she's former CIA."

"Yeah, right."

"She's got training. She's something."

The guy with the first aid kit got to work, staunching the wound and binding it with expert hands. I guessed he was ex-army too. He also gave the bouncer a shot of morphine for the pain.

The whole procedure took only a couple of minutes, a proper field dressing done with a skill and speed most civilian EMTs couldn't match. Just who was I dealing with here? He stood up and studied me.

"What do we do with her?" the man with the gun on me asked. His aim hadn't wavered. His arm looked like it was made of stone.

"Kill her!" Lance groaned.

"Shut up," the medic said. He turned to me. "Talk."

"I'd rather not, thank you."

"You want to get hurt, grandma?" he said, taking a step forward.

My wrists already throbbed from the impact. I wouldn't be able to hold a teacup steady for a couple of days at least.

"Torturing a former CIA officer will get you the electric chair, assuming my colleagues don't decide to take matters into their own hands. Besides, I've faced much worse than you."

The medic drew closer, his soulless eyes boring into mine. He nodded slowly.

"Yeah. Yeah, I think you have. But you haven't faced the Exterminator."

Oh dear. That was said with capital letters. I didn't want to meet this Exterminator fellow.

The guy pointing the gun at me chuckled. "You ever see *La Femme Nikita*? The original French version, not the crappy American remake?"

"Are we really going to discuss French cinema at a time like this?" I asked.

"Have you?"

"Yes."

"Remember the character of Victor?"

Oh dear. Oh deary me. That acid bathtub scene was not something easily forgotten.

A loud metallic thud came from the back room. The two thugs looked at each other, eyes wide. I guessed it wasn't the Exterminator.

There was another thud, and the bang of a door flying open and hitting the wall.

"Police!"

The medic sprinted for the open office door, gun blazing. I dropped to my knees and punched the gunman covering me in a place I'd normally never touch. He yelped, and his pistol went off, the sound jabbing my ears.

I gave the man another punch in the same spot that doubled him over. I scooped up my discarded pistol and shot him in the face.

Yes, I went for a killing shot. He would have never surrendered.

The medic stood behind the partially dismantled roulette table taking shots at someone in the back room. The return fire was sporadic, as if the cop was cowed and unsure what to do.

I adjusted my glasses, which had slipped off my nose in the rush, and took aim at the medic.

At the last moment, he glanced over his shoulder, saw me, and ducked. My bullet couldn't have missed him by more than an inch, but it missed him. He snapped an unaimed shot back at me that sent me diving behind a table, which I quickly upturned to make a shield.

Actually, I didn't dive behind the table. I made a sad little trot and knelt down on creaking knees, and my back twinged terribly as I upturned the table, which was of cheap material I seriously doubted would stop anything with a greater caliber than a BB gun.

I heard the telltale snap of a magazine being changed. I popped up—okay, eased up—and took another shot, but he'd wedged himself behind the solid oak roulette table in such a way that he was hidden from me and the cop in the back room. My bullet thumped into the wood but didn't pass through.

"Come out with your hands up!" the policeman ordered. "You're surrounded."

I recognized Police Chief Grimal's voice. That did not make me feel much better. The way he had blundered into this situation didn't give me any more confidence in his fighting ability than I had before, and I seriously doubted he had brought along any backup after who knows how long trying to cover this place up.

"Let us walk out of here, and the old lady won't get hurt!" the medic shouted.

"Don't listen to him," I called. "I'm safe and armed. He's stalling. He has backup coming."

A bullet chewed off the edge of my table. I cringed and dared a peek just in time to see the medic pop out from behind his own to take another shot. I fired and missed. At least it made him keep his head down.

Ten years ago, I would have taken the opportunity to leap up, send another couple of shots his way to keep him down, and shift to a better position, one that would offer me more protection and a better line of sight. That wasn't going to happen in this gunfight. Already, my knees were screaming with agony at having to kneel on the thin carpeting, and my leaping up and running days were over.

Then Grimal did something stupid. Maybe it was all those years of knowing he was inadequate, all those years of seeing big-city cops getting medals for bravery. Or maybe it was the pent-up guilt of having covered up this whole sordid affair for reasons I still didn't fully understand. Or maybe he was just stupid. For whatever reason, he came bursting out of the doorway like he was the sheriff in some Western movie, gun blazing.

Except you can't blaze when you only have a six-shot revolver you've already been firing. He fired once, twice, not even aiming, and then his gun made that awful click you never want to hear from someone on your own side in battle.

The medic and I popped up simultaneously.

I fired a fraction of a second before he did.

The shot hit the medic in the side, sending him flying and landing him hard on the floor, but not before he squeezed off a round that lodged in Grimal's shoulder.

The cop staggered. To his credit, he stayed on his feet, took a few stumbling steps over to the man I had just shot, and stepped on the medic's gun arm to immobilize it. His caution was unnecessary. The man was obviously dying.

Grimal picked up the medic's gun. A motion near the front of the room made us both turn.

Lance, the bouncer, rose up, eyes bleary with the morphine he'd been given, trying to aim down the sights of the gun he'd picked up.

Grimal and I shot him at the same time.

As the man slumped to the floor, the corrupt police chief and I both half turned toward each other, guns still drawn.

We paused. Neither offered to put their gun away first.

"Explain yourself," I demanded.

"I was investigating—"

"You were covering up for your brother-in-law. You turned the other way and covered up a murder so these loan sharks would forgive his debt."

"No! I didn't know a thing about it until he came to me for help. He'd been trying to hide his debts, applying for more and more credit cards to cover it up so my sister wouldn't know a thing. And then Archibald Heaney got murdered, and they leaned on him to declare it a suicide. That's when he came to me. I told him to do what he was told, let them wipe off the debt, and act like everything was okay so I could investigate. That's why he hasn't been coming to the casino, so he wouldn't be in the line of fire when everything went down."

I snorted. He said "everything went down" like every bad cop movie I'd ever seen. This guy was something else.

"Investigate?" I scoffed. "You only showed up when they were ready to skip town. You probably figured out I didn't believe your phony story and was going to investigate this case on my own. You only came in as damage control."

"No, you got to believe me. I wanted to do what was right, but I didn't want my brother-in-law to get hurt."

We still stood in that ridiculous position, half turned to each other with our guns leveled, aiming at nothing. He swayed on his feet. Blood flowed freely down his arm and side.

"You got to believe me," he repeated.

I sighed. As a matter of fact, I did believe him. If he had truly wanted to cover things up, he would have wiped away those footprints. He would have taken the time to make up a better cover story. What he should have done was call in the state police for help. Instead, he had tried to do everything himself and ended up doing everything the wrong way, but he had done it for family. This weak, ineffectual man had only been trying to save his sister some heartache. There were probably kids involved too.

"Put that gun down," I demanded. He was too stupid to be trusted.

He did as he was told, laying it on the nearest table with a heavy thud as if it weighed a hundred pounds. With that wounded shoulder, it probably felt that heavy.

"Come on," I said in a gentler voice. "Let's get you to a hospital."

He only nodded, not meeting my eye. Luckily, he still had enough strength to make it out the back door on his own. I wouldn't have been able to support his weight.

There was no police cruiser parked out back, only Grimal's private vehicle. I shook my head in disgust. A cop with secrets to hide is no cop worthy of the name.

He had tried to save my life, though. That counted for something.

A sedan rolled slowly around the corner. Instinctively, I raised my pistol. Anonymity be damned. This was survival.

Through the window, I saw a rugged face obscured by sunglasses. The man didn't flinch at the sight of a gun pointed at him. Instead, he turned the car around and drove out of sight.

I was tempted to fire, but I could not be one

hundred percent sure I wouldn't be firing at a civilian.

The last look the driver gave me told me my hunch was correct.

I'd just seen the Exterminator.

I didn't bother to note the make and model of the car or the license plate. It was stolen anyway, and he'd be long gone before the Cheerville flatfoots could trace him. Besides, I sensed that even if the town's entire police force cornered him, he'd come out alive.

Not anyone else, just him.

My gut feelings are almost always correct. Sometimes that's not a good thing.

The Exterminator had "professional" written all over him. I hoped he was professional enough to cut his losses and know not to come back to Cheerville again. There was no profit in messing with me.

I hoped.

ELEVEN

"Grandma's got a boyfriend! Grandma's got a boyfriend!" Martin announced in a singsong voice when I brought him back to his parents' house the following day. My knees and wrists still hurt from the fight. My ego hurt too, knowing Grimal had gotten all the credit for the bust. I had decided to continue being anonymous.

My daughter-in-law, Alicia, smiled and said, "Aw, isn't that sweet," in a voice you'd use if you heard your fifth grader had gotten a boyfriend.

My son, Frederick, got an uncomfortable look on his face and asked, "Is this true?" in a voice you'd use if you heard your eleventh grader had spent the night at her boyfriend's house.

"He's just a friend," I replied. My tone came out a bit too defensive to be convincing.

"I see," Frederick said, still sounding like the concerned parent.

"They were kissing," Martin said, making a smoochy face.

I blushed. Frederick blushed. Alicia rolled her eyes and turned away. Martin looked triumphant.

"I hope he wasn't too much trouble?" my son asked.

I presumed he meant Martin and not my "boyfriend."

"No, he's been wonderful as usual, although a bit prone to telling tall tales."

"You sure? You look worn out. You're not coming down with something, are you?" My son had become overly concerned with my health since I'd hit seventy, although I was in as good a shape as anyone could expect at my age.

"Oh, I'm just a bit tired. It's been a long few days."

"Sorry. I really appreciate it," Frederick said.

I let him think I meant Martin and not a murder investigation. A few guilt points are always handy to have with your son, even if he is a grown man.

"Will you stay for dinner?" Alicia called from the kitchen. "Frederick is making meat loaf."

I suppressed a shudder. I'd rather face down another gang of loan sharks than brave the terrors of my son's meat loaf. Poor Martin, although I guessed he deserved it for spilling the beans on me and Octavian.

"No, thank you. I already have some food prepared, and I think I'll turn in early. Plus, I have someone I need to see."

"Oooh," came Martin's voice from the couch. He was blasting aliens on the Xbox but remarkably still listening to our conversation. Usually when he played video games, he really was on another planet. "She's going to see her boyfriend!"

"Martin!" Alicia shouted from the kitchen. What she said next got drowned out by the blender. She sounded like she was crushing ice for a margarita. After such a long trip and the prospect of facing her husband's meat loaf, she needed one.

"No, I'm seeing someone else," I declared and then said goodbye.

What I didn't mention was that I'd see Octavian later for a drink of our own. But first, I needed to pay a visit to Police Chief Grimal.

I found him in his office, looking guarded and downcast. His arm was in a sling.

I closed the door behind me and sat down opposite him without being invited and gave him the Look.

The Look—always capitalized both in its written and spoken form, just like the Exterminator—is something cultivated by all CIA operatives. We actually practice it on each other and do it in front of the mirror until we get it right. The Look can change with the situation. You don't use the same Look on some low-level narcotrafficker as you would on an international assassin, but the Look always says more or less the same thing—"I don't care if you live or die, but I'm going to make damn sure you do what I tell you."

It helps if the recipient of the Look knows you're CIA. Police Chief Grimal did.

So I used the Look. I didn't say anything, I just Looked.

And Looked.

He visibly wilted. He knew he was in trouble, as much trouble as I wanted to put him in. I could ruin his life forever. His brother-in-law's life too.

But I wasn't going to. Because in the end, Grimal had only been protecting his family. He'd done it in a stupid way, a sloppy way, a way that nearly got himself and me killed, but his motives had been good ones.

I raised a forefinger.

"You get one more chance."

Grimal looked up at me, hope sparking in his eyes.

"But you have to remember one thing."

"What's that?"

I turned my hand downward and pressed it against the nameplate on his desk, making it fall over with a clack. I pressed harder. My fingertip landed on the word "Chief."

"From now on, you're my tool. You understand? You do what I tell you, nothing more, nothing less, and if I catch you messing up again…"

I flicked the nameplate across the desk. It bounced off his gut and clattered to the floor.

I got up and walked out of the office without another word.

After that, I went home and fed Dandelion, worked in the garden for a little while, and then went out for a lovely cup of tea with Octavian.

ABOUT THE AUTHOR

Harper Lin is the *USA TODAY* bestselling author of 6 cozy mystery series including *The Patisserie Mysteries* and *The Cape Bay Cafe Mysteries*.

When she's not reading or writing mysteries, she loves going to yoga classes, hiking, and hanging out with her family and friends.

www.HarperLin.com

66432146R00090

Made in the USA
Lexington, KY
13 August 2017